Villages where
Jacques lived

Enemy
villages

Overland Trail

New fort

Old fort

Spanish
fort

Massacre Island

Florida

Gulf
of
Mexico

Course of the Palm Tree and Renown.

THE PAINTED ARROW

THE
PAINTED ARROW

By
FRANCES GAITHER

Illustrated by
HENRY PITZ

NEW YORK
THE JUNIOR LITERARY GUILD
1931

To Captain Jack

CONTENTS

CONTENTS

ILLUSTRATIONS

THE PAINTED ARROW

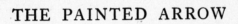

CHAPTER I

THE WALLED GARDEN

THE garden smelled of ripe peaches and roses and honeysuckle. Susanne, the yellow cat, was asleep on the graveled path, and Jacques had to step over her as he passed out of the kitchen door into the late sunlight. The parrot, with his gray plumage and red tail, sat in his cage in the plum-tree, chattering away in that African language of his.

Against the sunny bricks where the peaches hung, leaned the upper half of a woman's body carved in oak and bleached by salt-spray. Jacques looked at it sadly. It had been the figurehead of his father's boat, the *Swallow*, and was all that was left of the *Swallow* now. At the foot of the path beyond the raspberry bushes, grew a tall cactus from the Indies. With its queer un-

dersea color and its cruel claws, it always made Jacques
think of some strange monster.   Against the south wall,
among the roses and honeysuckle, was planted the jasmin vine from the Mississippi.   The jasmin and the
parrot and the cactus had been given to Jacques by various sailors he knew.

Often Jacques pretended that he himself was a sailor
and that these were the things he had brought home to
the little walled garden to remind him of this voyage
or that.   But now such a game seemed all at once silly
and childish.   He didn't even care about climbing the
tree he called the Mainmast, a tall linden growing by
the gate in the outer wall.

Inside the kitchen his father's voice still went on.
His father was talking now to Jacques' Aunt Gabrielle.

"I wonder," said the skipper crossly, "where that boy
got his tastes from—sitting here for hours by the table
inking up his fingers.   His mother was as active a body
as ever lived.   And I certainly never was one to sit
ashore writing my name with pretty flourishes in a
book."

That was true, of course.   Jacques' father couldn't
read or write at all.   He was what they called in that
part of France a sea-wolf.

"All the same," said Aunt Gabrielle with a note of
pride in her voice, "Jacques is the only boy in town the
priest thinks it worth while to teach."

The skipper said nothing to that.   His cane tapped
the kitchen flagging as he rose from his chair, and
Jacques heard him limping toward the door.   When he
came alongside Jacques in the garden he seemed to

notice that he had hurt Jacques' feelings. Anyway he hesitated a moment and coughed in embarrassment.

"I guess," he said in the tone of a man offering an apology, "it takes all sorts to make a world: scribblers as well as sailors."

Jacques couldn't speak. So he nodded instead. The skipper stumped on down the path, opened the gate to the street, and disappeared, tapping his cane along the cobbles outside.

Jacques' father was a wreck of a man. Everybody said he was lucky to be alive after that cruel storm which had beaten the *Swallow* to pieces off the rocky coast of Brittany. But when a man has spent his whole life going and coming upon the sea it's hard to be cast ashore so battered up as to be no longer good for anything—except to sit and hear other men tell where they have been or are going. The town was always filled with people waiting for ships to put to sea or with people returned from the sea and waiting for post-horses. There was always somebody ready to chat with an idle man at Little Sailor Inn or along the water-front. But the talk—about the New World, mostly—only made the disabled skipper the more restless and discontented. Maybe it was only natural he should find fault with Jacques for every little thing.

But Jacques missed the *Swallow*, too. It had been his father's habit almost ever since Jacques was born to take Jacques with him now and then on his journeys up and down the coast of France so that the boy might be seasoned to a sailor's life later on. But now Jacques had to spend his days shut up in the walled garden with nothing at all to do and no more cruises to look forward to.

Aunt Gabrielle came out of the house, sat down on a bench by the kitchen door with a wooden platter on her knees, and began to cut up cabbage for the evening soup. She looked toward Jacques sympathetically. But he didn't feel like talking. So he moved off down the path. The cat Susanne, suddenly awake, scurried ahead of him and whisked aloft the Mainmast to crouch as round and yellow as a big orange in the topmost leaves. Jacques smiled then, ran to the tree, kicked off his wooden shoes, and followed her up.

When he got to the crotch where Susanne lay waiting, Aunt Gabrielle showed doll-size by the low little house, and Jacques looked down into other gardens walled like his own and scattered like his with parts of wrecked ships and exotic plants and tropical birds. There was hardly a house in this town but was home to some captain or pilot or sailor when he was ashore, and from the house next door a boy no older than Jacques had run away to sea last spring. Perched in the Mainmast, Jacques overlooked not only the low walls of the gardens and houses but the great ramparts which encircled the town all ruffled with trees. He saw the river which flowed past the town between two wide green plains, out and out to the sea reddening now to sunset, with blue shadowy islands floating dim and far upon the colored water.

The river was brimming at this hour with the full tide. A pair of ruddy sails no bigger than a little red butterfly came fluttering in from the sea. Jacques watched the two square sails flying low over the river, and he thought wistfully of the poor little *Swallow*. Just before the town, at the foot of the king's towered arsenal, two tall ships lay at anchor. Men scurried like ants over their decks and among the rigging where the looped canvas glowed as pink as sea-shells in the sunset. The fresh-painted hulls were mirrored in the brimming, rosy river. They were the *Renown* and the *Palm Tree* making ready, with the little brig moored alongside, to sail for Louisiana, or the Mississippi, as some people called Monsieur d'Iberville's new little colony.

Monsieur d'Iberville was the man who last year had entered the mouth of the Mississippi, the vast, mysterious river of the New World, claiming it and the lands it watered for the king of France. Monsieur d'Iberville was a hero to Jacques, as to many another boy in this town, and those two ships of his were bathed in a glory that was more than the rose of this brief sunset.

Jacques sat in his treetop looking at the ships in the river until wheels and hoofs came clattering over the cobbles below him. He looked down and saw rolling past his garden gate a fine carriage all blue paint and gilded carving, with a dozen curious urchins clattering behind it in their wooden sabots. Whereupon Jacques forgot all about the ships. A minute more and he was outside the gate running along with the rest.

CHAPTER II

At Little Sailor Inn

In the courtyard of Little Sailor Inn a gentleman in a plumed hat and buckled shoes with red heels got out of the carriage. He took snuff from a jeweled snuff-box and scolded about the condition of the roads while one of the inn boys wiped with his apron the fine buckled shoes. Then the gentleman went indoors. While the grooms were taking the horses out and wiping the dust

6

from the gilded wheels, Jacques learned that the gentleman had come all the way from the palace at Versailles with orders from the king for Monsieur d'Iberville. And one of the grooms offered to bet Jacques and the inn stable-boy that the *Renown* and the *Palm Tree* would be going out on to-morrow's tide.

Jacques slipped inside the inn through a door open on the courtyard. He planned to say he was looking for his father if anybody should try to stop him. But nobody did. The whole place was in such bustle and stir that a boy more or less under foot made no difference. He passed unquestioned through the kitchen and the room beyond that and out into the garden. Even Monsieur Bosset, the inn-keeper, paid no attention to him. Monsieur Bosset stood with his napkin over his arm close by a table under the trees at which sat Monsieur d'Iberville and the king's courier.

On the table between the two men lay a map with red and black markings; on top of it, the king's dispatches to Monsieur d'Iberville all tied with red and green silk fastened with big seals of green wax; and in a little huddle some curiosities which Monsieur d'Iberville had brought from Louisiana and was about to send to Versailles. There were arrowheads chipped out of flint; a bit of green earth which might contain copper; a little earthen bowl patterned with red and black; a ball of buffalo wool spun by savages, that looked for all the world like good French wool; a chaplet of curious shell-beads; and a pipe with a bowl carved and painted in the semblance of some grotesque god and with a stem nearly a yard long trailing feather streamers like a lady's fan.

When Monsieur d'Iberville talked he touched these various things with his strong blunt fingers, and that made the experiences he recounted seem oddly real.

"All the principal chiefs sang the calumet to me," said Monsieur d'Iberville. He lifted the strange barbaric pipe, although it was empty, and touched it to his lips with a faint reminiscent smile. "I gave them bells and mirrors and a blanket apiece from his Majesty."

There came into Jacques' mind a vision of a dark and shadowed forest and naked princes greeting with their strange ceremonies Monsieur d'Iberville in his naval officer's uniform with the cross of St. Louis sparkling on his breast. All the far country outlined under Monsieur d'Iberville's great palm came into Jacques' mind while Monsieur d'Iberville was talking. There was an island called Massacre because of bones whitening in the sand. There were dim mysterious rivers leading men deeper and deeper into forests so thick that to pass through them one must chop out paths and use always two hands at once to part the tangle. There were everywhere savages creeping through the trees, slipping along the rivers in dugouts. There were villages loath to give up their secrets to white men.

The king's messenger took a pinch of snuff out of his fine snuff-box, brushed out his lace jabot with slender white fingers and said, yawning slightly:

"But, my dear Iberville, surely it wasn't wise to drop your handful of followers on such a savage coast. They'll only be butchered like the poor souls La Salle put ashore in the same region. You found no pearls, anyway," the courtier went on, "no gold mines, no ambergris. I can't see that your adventure has any value—except perhaps to a geographer."

Here the white fingers dropped and flicked the map, trailing disdainful laces across the charted seas. Monsieur d'Iberville's big nostrils widened, his level lips twitched slightly.

"Fortunately," he said, "there are those who do not agree with you—his Majesty for one."

And he began to gather into packets the things that lay upon the table. When he spoke again it was in a hard, cold voice not at all the same in which he had talked about his New World. He directed the courtier dryly what to tell the king and the minister of the marine when he should get back to Versailles: the *Renown* and the *Palm Tree* with their companion brig would sail to-morrow as ordered. They were armed. He still thought the crew of fifty for the *Palm Tree* too small, but since Versailles counted on the passengers helping in emergencies there was no more to be said on that score. He'd take on another good carpenter or so if any could be found in the morning. And he still lacked a ship's boy. The lists of the supplies he was taking were here in this smaller packet. Enough for seven months only—if Monsieur will be so good as to call his Majesty's attention. A ship should be sent to arrive at the end of that time. It would be well to send then some girls, as pretty as possible, to be married to the men and make homes for them. The colony should have at least one great strong stallion. And Spanish sheep—please ask his Majesty to take note— have wool that is longer and finer than the wool on French sheep.

"Monsieur! Monsieur!"

Jacques jumped. The inn-keeper's voice, like that
of many fat men, had a shrill quality anyway, and now,
suddenly interrupting Monsieur d'Iberville's resonant
one, it squeaked like the cry of a frightened small animal.

"Monsieur, are inn-keepers needed, too, in your colony at the Mississippi?"

The gentleman from the court laughed. So, unluckily did Jacques. Monsieur Bosset turned on
Jacques and angrily flapped his napkin.

All his life long Jacques was to remember that scene
in the twilit summer evening outside Little Sailor Inn—
the table piled with its maps of a New World, and ribboned court documents all mixed up anyhow with Indian
beads and feathers; Monsieur d'Iberville sitting erect
in his naval officer's uniform with the king's decoration
pinned on his breast; the mocking courtier from Versailles whose laces gleamed like foam in the dusk; poor
Monsieur Bosset the inn-keeper, with a face all white
and drawn in fear at the words he had spoken, flapping
a snowy napkin at Jacques because Jacques had laughed,
and squealing in his funny fat man's voice, "Be off, you
young rascal, be off."

Running home through the darkening streets Jacques
felt sorry for Monsieur Bosset. It was one thing for
men like Monsieur d'Iberville to go on strange and
dangerous voyages. But there was something absurd
about Monsieur Bosset's even wanting to go. Suppose
he should go. Suppose he should be captured by the
savages. Why, he would have no more chance than
the white-handed courtier or—Jacques smiled—the cat
Susanne.

Jacques was still thinking of Monsieur Bosset when he ran in through the garden. He started when something leaned out of the shadows and laid a savage claw upon his cheek. He knew it was only the cactus and yet he ran toward the house, his heart thumping. Through the open door came out to him gently wavering candle-light, the smell of good cabbage soup, and the voices of his father and his Aunt Gabrielle in peaceful chat.

"The *Renown* and the *Palm Tree* have the king's orders to sail, and they're needing a ship's boy!"

His aunt and his father looked around as if they had not understood a word he had said. It is no wonder they were astonished. To himself his voice sounded less like his own than like Monsieur Bosset's, all awry with terror and daring. The skipper took no more notice of his son's news than if Jacques had spoken it in the gibberish their parrot used. And all Aunt Gabrielle said was:

"Why, Jacques, you've cut your cheek. My poor darling. Let Aunt Gabrielle see."

"I just ran into the cactus," he told her impatiently and wrenched his shoulders out of her grasp to fling himself at his father.

"It's to-morrow they're sailing, *to-morrow*—and they want a ship's boy."

Still the skipper didn't seem to hear. And Jacques, suddenly, was rather relieved that he didn't. He turned back toward his aunt, his hand against his cheek.

"It was dark in the garden," he began, but his father cut him short:

"When is it they're sailing?"

"To-morrow, but—"

"And they want a ship's boy?"

"Yes—but of course I don't know how old a boy they want or—"

"But they do need a boy?"

"Yes."

There wasn't a sound for a long while but the soup murmuring in the pot hanging on its crane and the faggots crackling underneath. The skipper sat looking at his son, taking his measure. Jacques shifted his feet nervously. Of course he was going to sea someday. He always had meant to. But after all there was no hurry about it.

"He's only a child," begged Aunt Gabrielle.

"Well," said the battered skipper at last, "I can't believe Monsieur d'Iberville would give the place to him. The boy isn't what I'd call properly seasoned yet, by a good deal."

The skipper paused a moment. And Jacques, pulled this way and that by fear and desire, said in a shrill, eager voice that sounded in his own ears like somebody else's:

"You'll ask him, Father?"

"I'll ask him," the skipper promised, "in the morning. And I'd be glad if he thought he could make a seaman of you—seeing I've no chance now to do the job myself. A lad of spirit's in a fair way to be ruined if he keeps ashore with women and priests."

Aunt Gabrielle began to cry.

CHAPTER III

A Seaman's Chest

Although Jacques and his father were up and out early next morning, the river-front was already thronging. It looked as if the king's entire magazine were being emptied to fit out the *Renown* and the *Palm Tree*. Cart after cart dumped boxes and kegs on the quay and rattled off for another load. Little boats borne low in the water with freight hurried from wharf edge to ship side and, as soon as they were emptied, back to wharf edge again.   The pulleys on shipboard creaked unceasingly, hoisting cases and bales over the sides into the holds.

Even when Jacques and his father found Monsieur d'Iberville at last, they had to wait their turn to speak to him.   Jacques was terribly impatient.   What if one of those men ahead of them should claim for his own son the place Jacques now coveted with all his heart? Monsieur d'Iberville was answering questions and giving orders and all the while dictating to a young man who was using an overturned keg for a desk:

"Five hundred large, small, and medium-sized hatchets.   Bird-shot, sail-cloth, tents.   Five hundred pounds of glass beads—purple, white, red, and mixed.   Twenty-five gross of little bells.   Eight pounds of vermilion. Ten scarlet hats with tinsel braid and sham plumes."

All about him pressed passengers demanding to know the hour of sailing, workmen with orders to be signed, weathered Canadian soldiers, young midshipmen in brand new uniforms with shining buttons, sailors clamoring for instructions.   Among the rest was a young woman in a blue hooded cape who told Jacques' father she wanted to get permission to sail aboard one of the ships.

"The place for women is ashore," the skipper told her severely.   But all the same he drew Jacques aside to let her pass ahead of them.

Jacques felt sorry for the girl whose eyes so blue under her hood seemed to him to be full of trouble, and, impatient as he was, he was glad his father let her go first.   When the girl moved on with the permit she wanted, Monsieur d'Iberville turned to Jacques' father.

"And now, my good man," he said, "what can I do for you?"

The skipper limped forward and with his seaman's bluntness stated their business in a sentence.

"My son here heard you say last night, Monsieur, that you need a ship's boy; and, being a lad of spirit with a thirst to see the world, he wants the place."

Here Monsieur d'Iberville was interrupted to talk to a young workman in a red beret who had heard carpenters were wanted. And then he had to talk with the pilot of the *Palm Tree*. But he sought among the papers at his secretary's elbow on the overturned keg and handed to the skipper one which Jacques had certainly seen before. Jacques recognized at once the red and green silk ties, and at the edge, broken now, the royal seal of green wax.

"That will explain everything to you," said Monsieur d'Iberville. "Just be so good as to look it over and I'll talk to you in a minute."

The skipper stared at the mysterious writing and then handed the document to Jacques.

"What does it say?" he whispered uneasily.

The document went to Jacques' head like wine. It began, "Louis by the grace of God King of France and of Navarre, to Pierre Le Moyne, Sieur d'Iberville, greetings. We have received your dispatches and We desire . . . " The high phrases swept deliciously down the page, the loops of the *L*'s and *Y*'s flowing around the great *W* of that august, recurrent *We* like the sweeping skirts of ladies-in-waiting curtsying to the king. Jacques was so overcome to be holding in his hand a letter from the king that he could hardly read it. To make it all the harder his father kept hurrying him.

"Leave out the frills, Jacques. Leave out the frills."

Below the king's message the king's minister had written:

"His Majesty finds it good that you shall embark the wives and daughters—"

"Leave out the women, Jacques. What does it say about a ship's boy?"

"With regard to a boy to serve the workers at sea and ashore—"

"Shore duty!" fumed the skipper. "That's always the trouble about shipping to the colonies."

"I shan't mind," Jacques put in quickly, thinking of a place called Massacre Island and strange rivers and secret villages. "I'd like that!"

The looped letters of the next sentence made a tangle. It seemed to be all about duties. It didn't interest Jacques. Anyway his eyes lit a little further on upon the most enticing list in the world. He just skipped the sentence about duties—what any other boy could do he could—and read instead what the document said about rewards:

"His Majesty agrees that you employ such a boy at the usual wage, and the king's magazine may furnish him with the following outfit: four shirts at forty sous apiece . . . "

The catalogue of the outfit item by item filled ten

lines. Jacques read it aloud slowly. At the end he met his father's eyes and perceived in them a solemn pride.

"It's hard to believe the king would think worth while," the skipper marveled, "to give so much to a slip of a boy who knows, you might say, less than nothing yet."

Monsieur d'Iberville beckoned them forward, but a narrow-visaged man dressed in costly though shabby clothes elbowed past and himself addressed Monsieur d'Iberville. He demanded, in a fawning and insistent way, a letter to the king.

"But, Monsieur," Monsieur d'Iberville objected, "I have told you I will write back from the West Indies. There is not a minute to spare now for selfish interests. Besides, my final dispatches have just gone."

The other rubbed his palms and said ingratiatingly:

"I detained your courier, my dear Iberville. The matter is most urgent. Believe me—"

"You stopped the courier! But, really, Monsieur—"

"I must have more money. I must, my dear Iberville. Fifty pounds is a pittance. Think of my services to France. Think of my large family. And my wife —surely my wife should have some reward, the first woman to go out to the Mississippi—you say yourself your colony needs women, my dear Iberville."

The harassed d'Iberville turned to his secretary and with a slight shrug dictated a request to the king that his Majesty augment the salary of his newly appointed commissary to the colony at the Mississippi. The royal commissary had a large family—

"And my wife," the insistent commissary interrupted.

"Put in my wife, my dear Iberville.   And while you're about it you might mention that I married her at the suggestion of Madame, the Grand Duchess—you probably don't realize the importance of that, but it will have a lot of influence at court—ah, thanks, a thousand thanks, my dear fellow.   Now if you'll kindly sign that I'll hand it over to the king's messenger so you'll be put to no further trouble—"   Bowing low, the royal commissary withdrew at last.

"There is a man," Jacques' father observed in a whisper, "that Monsieur d'Iberville would do better to leave behind.   He belongs ashore with his letter-writing and his schemes."

"Well," Monsieur d'Iberville addressed the skipper. "Now that you see what I want, do you still want me to take your son?"

Jacques wet his lips.

"If you please, Monsieur," he cried before his father had time to speak.

Monsieur d'Iberville smiled.

"So you really are a lad of spirit, are you?"

"He is that, Monsieur," the skipper declared.   "And young as he is, he's a bit seasoned to the sea and its ways."

Monsieur d'Iberville looked hard at Jacques as last night his father had looked at him.   Jacques could hardly breathe.

"Assign this boy to the *Palm Tree*," Monsieur d'Iberville said at last to the young man scribbling on the overturned keg.

That gentleman took Jacques' name and made a copy

of the magic list for him as though it were all the most natural business in the world.   At the magazine, too, the order was taken out of Jacques' hand and speedily filled in the most commonplace and matter-of-fact fashion.   But neither Jacques nor his father could treat the affair lightly.   They spread down the good warm blanket upon a table and the skipper counted the things on to it while Jacques read the list again item by item:

> One blanket
> Four shirts
> Two pairs of stockings
> Two pairs of leather shoes
> One suit of clothes
> One jacket
> One cloth cap
> Two suits of underwear
> Leather leggings, thread, needles
>   and various other trifles
> One hammock

They counted the outfit twice over and then they rolled everything together neatly in the blanket.   It made a rather large packet.   The skipper offered to help Jacques carry it.   But Jacques wouldn't give it up. He hugged it to him as they made their way out of the magazine.   Everywhere they looked they saw provisions destined for the outgoing ships: kegs of oil and wine from the great cellars, boxes of biscuits and salted meat, sacks of peas and flour and rice.   As they came out upon the quay two men trotted past carrying a bale of brilliantly colored blankets.

"Look," cried Jacques, "presents for the Indians."

But his father was watching a crowd of sailors struggling with a flock of sheep, tying their feet to load them into a boat.   Above the bleating of the sheep and the panic of poultry the skipper's voice rang out in admiration:

"There'll be no going ragged or hungry on Monsieur d'Iberville's ships, eh, Jacques?"

Even Aunt Gabrielle was immensely cheered when she saw what they had brought.   She had never seen such a wardrobe.   Jacques had never had even one pair of leather shoes before or a single new coat or new breeches.   He wore sabots of course, and Aunt Gabrielle had always cut down his father's pea-jackets and breeches for him, all dim and faded with salt-spray as they were.   When she saw all his bright new things, she was filled with pride of Jacques and gratitude to the king.

"He's fitted you out like a young lord," she said as she folded and refolded the four fine shirts and the jacket with the bright buttons.   "Surely the king's own grandson, the young Duke of Anjou, going down to be king of Spain, could have had no finer clothes than these."

The skipper brought out his own chest for her to pack Jacques' things in—a real seaman's chest that had been on more voyages than its owner had ever troubled to count.   It was covered with a piece of stout old sail-cloth, well tarred and marked with the skipper's mark, an anchor painted red and black and so designed as to conceal by curves and embellishments the awkwardness of the initials on the shank. The skipper apologized to Jacques for the clumsy lettering. "Not much like the writing they do at court, eh, Jacques?" But, the truth was, all the fine flourishes of the king's minister could not have made Jacques any prouder than he already was of that seaman's chest.

CHAPTER IV

The Palm Tree Puts to Sea

Last of all Aunt Gabrielle slipped in between the folded shirts the saint's medal she had bought that morning from a passing peddler and got the priest to bless. It was silver, embossed with the image of the good saint carrying a boy on his shoulder across water. Little silver waves beat up to the saint's knees, but he held the boy high and safe above them. When Aunt Gabrielle had finished packing the chest, she kindled the faggots in the chimney and made a last omelet for Jacques while his father locked the chest and roped it well. After that, they started, Jacques and his father carrying the chest between them, Aunt Gabrielle carrying Susanne.

"Susanne wants to see Jacques sail, don't you, Susanne?" poor Aunt Gabrielle said foolishly, her mouth all twisted with trying to smile when she really felt more like crying.

When they came out upon the river-front there was Monsieur Bosset, the inn-keeper, his familiar fat form wrapped in a most unfamiliar black traveling cloak. He hurried forward to greet them, his broad black hat pressed under his arm; and when he heard that Jacques was joining the expedition he was flatteringly delighted. Last night seemed to be as remote to Monsieur Bosset

now as it was to Jacques.   The good little inn-keeper
was in high feather and as full of great concerns as
Monsieur d'Iberville himself.

"And madame, your wife, how does she stand your
leaving her?" asked Aunt Gabrielle.

Monsieur Bosset's shining face clouded over.
Jacques could hardly keep from laughing at him again.
He looked as though he were about to burst into tears
standing there with his short fat legs thrust wide apart
beneath that strange long cloak.

"Ah, the poor soul."   He gave a sigh which was all
but a sob.   "Yonder she stands crying her eyes out.
Do be so good as to say a kind word to her, Mademoiselle."

Aunt Gabrielle moved over to offer poor Madame
Bosset what consolation she could.   Jacques' father
went away with Monsieur Bosset to find out whether
Monsieur Bosset's name was listed for the *Renown* or
the *Palm Tree*.   Susanne curled up on the chest and
Jacques sat down beside her.

A carriage clattered up and discharged onto the quay
the royal commissary to the colony at the Mississippi;
his lady, a delicate-appearing woman with a high, complaining voice; several children; and a great number of
trunks and boxes and parcels of every sort and size.
The commissary dismissed the carriage with a flourish
of his ribboned cane and went off afoot along the quay
on some errand or other.   His lady hoisted a ruffled
sunshade, and, spreading her flowered brocade skirts,
sat down on a trunk in the midst of their chattels, where
she occupied herself scolding her children.

The eldest, a boy near Jacques' own age, with a narrow face like the father's and the same unquiet black eyes, walked over to where Jacques sat with Susanne on his lap.   The chest seemed to interest the commissary's son.   He walked around it several times staring at it. Then he stooped to study the anchor with its crude letters painted on the end.

"Who painted that?" he asked.

"My father."

"He doesn't know how to write, does he?"

All the blood in Jacques' body flew into his face leaving his hands and feet like ice.

"No.   He is a sea-wolf.   Why should he sit ashore and ink up his fingers like some boys' fathers?"

"You mean mine?"   The other boy was surprised.

"Yes."

Jacques pushed Susanne off his knees and stood up. He wanted the commissary's son to hit him.   He wanted it with all his heart.   His cold fingers doubled up tight in his palms.   But the other boy just backed off, his sharp little nose quivering into a sneer.

"So your father is a sea-wolf, is he?   Well, it just happens mine has served in the king's navy for fourteen years.   And he happened to be with La Salle when he went down the Mississippi River before you were born."

Jacques was quite taken aback.   Was it possible that the commissary was a brave and adventurous gentleman after all?   Could Jacques' father have been mistaken in his judgment of him?

The commissary returned to his family just then, and his son evidently reported to him his skirmish with

Jacques, for the commissary looked Jacques' way and laughed unpleasantly.   He had brought along with him three sailors who shouldered the family's luggage and began to load it in a little canopied boat waiting by the edge of the quay.   After the luggage was stowed, the commissary, whom the sailors called Monsieur Nicolas, helped his wife and children in, and the sailors took up their oars.

As soon as the canopied boat had pulled out into the river, an open boat drew into the quay, and a sailor standing up in the prow to fling out a looped rope and make it fast called out to Jacques:

"Where does that chest go, my lad?"

"Aboard the *Palm Tree*," answered Jacques, his heart beginning to beat so hard it almost suffocated him.

Things happened very fast then.   Aunt Gabrielle, seeing the sailors taking Jacques' chest away, came hurrying back to him.   And his father got there at the same moment with Monsieur Bosset, who hastily kissed his wife good-by and stepped right down into the boat where Jacques' chest was being stowed, calling back:

"Come along, Jacques, my boy.   We're to be ship-mates, you see."

The young woman for whom Jacques had felt sorry that morning came running up, her blue hood awry, her cape blowing about her.   She did not have any chest or trunk but carried her belongings tied up in a big kerchief with tiny sprigs of pink flowers all over it.   She looked down at the low little boat and then out to the towering *Palm Tree*.

"Oh, how shall I ever get aboard?" she said.

"We'll tie you in a blanket," a sailor told her, "and hoist you up on a pulley like any other bale of goods."

The other sailors laughed, and the girl blushed. The young carpenter in the red beret stepped up to her side and said:

"Don't you mind them, Mademoiselle. Sailors must have their joke. Look yonder."

Out in the river the canopied boat had now drawn alongside the *Palm Tree,* and at this moment madame, the lady of the royal commissary, was riding slowly upward seated commodiously in a little armchair swing, her sunshade folded across her knees, her brocaded skirts fluttering discreetly about her ankles.

"Oh," breathed the girl in relief and without another word let the sailors hand first her bundle and then herself down into the open boat beside the quay.

The carpenter climbed down after her. He, too, carried a single parcel. It was, rather oddly, a violin case covered in sail cloth. Jacques to-day had seen very nearly every other sort of thing loaded aboard the ships bound for the New World, but nothing had struck him in quite the same fashion as the violin which the carpenter carried in his arms tenderly, as if it were a baby.

"Now, Jacques, my son," prompted the skipper.

Jacques was still holding Susanne. There came into his mind, most strangely, a picture of Susanne to-morrow alone in the garden with the chattering parrot and the carved figurehead of the *Swallow* and the jasmin and the cactus and the ripe peaches and the roses and the Mainmast—he wondered if Susanne would climb the Mainmast to-morrow alone. His clasped arms squeezed Susanne hard and would not let go.

"What is it, Jacques?" asked the skipper, puzzled.

The boat was ready to push off. Monsieur Bosset was seated in the stern looking back quite impatiently. The young woman in the blue hooded cape had sat down just in front of him, her flower-sprigged bundle on her knees. On the heaped-up baggage perched Jacques' chest, its red anchor uppermost. Two sailors were ready with their oars. The third was standing up in the bow to loose the rope and push off. The carpenter was standing up in the bow, too. He nodded his red cap and smiled at Jacques.

"Want to bring your cat along, boy?"

"Bring her along!" Jacques echoed.

"Well, why not? Don't you suppose there are rats and mice in Louisiana the same as there are in France?"

The sailors laughed, and one of them said:

"Bring her along if you like, boy."

When the *Renown* fired her signal gun at last and turned about in the river, and the *Palm Tree* with the little brig close behind moved out after her, the crowd along the quay waved and cheered. Jacques stood at the rail of the *Palm Tree* and watched the white starched wings of Aunt Gabrielle's cap dwindle to the size of butterfly's wings and then vanish altogether. After the ship had rounded the first bend in the river he could still look back on the walled town across the plains, but it dwindled, too, at last until its tufted crown of trees was no bigger than a courtier's wig.

"Why, where's your cat?"

The red-capped carpenter leaned his elbows on the rail.

"I lost her," said Jacques biting his lip. "She jumped down an open hatch the minute we came aboard."

"Oh, then you'll find her. That's one thing about a ship—one can't wander far."

The carpenter's name was Picard, no, not Monsieur Picard, or even Jean or Baptiste Picard, just Picard. He had lived in Paris all his life, and he was going to the New World to seek his fortune. The girl in the blue hooded cape was standing just beyond. She told them her name was Marie. She came from Dieppe.

"Ever been to sea before?" she asked them.

Picard never had.

"I have," said Jacques. And he told them about the *Swallow*. "But," he suddenly considered, "I have never been on the open sea."

Ahead, the *Renown* had spread all her sails and was sweeping out of the mouth of the river. The river where it widened and all the sea ahead were rosy with the light of sunset, exactly as Jacques had seen it yesterday from the Mainmast. To the south lay Madame Island, straight in front the long familiar outlines of Oleron, and northward the Isle of Ré. Out beyond them was the ocean.

CHAPTER V

"Ship's Boy! Ship's Boy!"

THE *Renown* was the favored ship of the little fleet. She had the dignity of a full battery of fifty guns, and Monsieur d'Iberville himself was her captain. She was slenderly built and easy to sail. The battle-scarred *Palm Tree,* carrying forty-four guns and fitted out as store-ship was, by contrast, very cumbersome. She had a clumsy great mainyard and anchors of two thousand weight. They soon found it was as much as the *Palm Tree* could do, crowding all her sails, to keep up with the *Renown* carrying only her four large ones. There is nothing so likely to spoil a crew's temper as a stubborn and wayward ship. And the crew of the *Palm Tree,* being shorthanded besides, as Monsieur d'Iberville had vainly pointed out before they had set sail, considered themselves very hardly used and grumbled incessantly. They found fault with everything and everybody including Jacques, the ship's boy.

"Ship's boy, did you scrub that table or did you have your cat lick it?" "Ship's boy, the time you're needed is when you're called—not ten minutes later. Understand?" Sometimes they called him into the forecastle on the pretense of an errand to be done and then kept him there baiting him. "I hear you were a sailor once, ship's boy.   Tell us about the good ship *Swallow*.   Had she twenty sails now—or was it two?"   And then they would guffaw and shout, their bare feet swinging over the sides of their hammocks.

Jacques was used to sailors.   Their rough ways did not annoy him nearly so much as the officiousness of Monsieur Nicolas, going out to the colony to be royal commissary.   That gentleman, though he traveled as a passenger only, consorted with the naval and military officers aboard and claimed the services of Jacques, the ship's boy, oftener than any of them.   Sometimes the commissary sent his son to fetch Jacques.   "Ship's boy!" the black-eyed boy would sing out insolently. "Ship's boy, aft—and hurry up about it."

Off the coast of Spain the winds began to be contrary and held so the better part of two weeks.   This buffeting occasioned no mishap beyond some delay, of concern chiefly to sailors determined to grumble on every score.   The *Palm Tree* rode the wind out at last, held on its course, and weathered the island of Madeira.   It was then that Jacques began to see those little flying fish of which he had so often heard travelers tell.   These fish, when porpoises chase them, take a little flight of about a pistol shot and then fall in the sea again—or into a ship as it goes sailing by.   In these seas mariners relied on the mild and steady trade winds, but when the winds failed them they were often becalmed.   The ships from France had more than their share of calms, delayed now as much by too little wind as they had been at first by too much.

It was hot beyond Madeira.   The supplies with

THE WINDS BEGAN TO BE CONTRARY.

which the king had so richly dowered them began to spoil. Many a cask or keg burst apart and had to be flung in the sea. The flour got moldy. Much of the salt beef and bacon served to the men was unsound. Only the wine kept the flavor it had had when it had been packed in France, and even it was too warm to taste right.

"Ship's boy, that bread's not fit to eat. Feed it to the fishes and bring me another loaf." "If I've got to drink warm wine, I'll at least have a full ration—did you sip this on the way up, ship's boy? Speak up if you don't want a box on the jaw." "You know, fellows, this boy wants disciplining. When I was a ship's boy, they whipped us once a week to keep us nimble."

One hot night as Jacques ran barefoot along the deck a sailor padding along in front of him turned suddenly.

"So you'll throw things at me, will you, ship's boy?"

Below, the sea lay deep and dark like velvet except where the band of moon-spangles trimmed it; and high above reached the towering sails white under the moon. The sailor had no shirt on, and his skin glistened with sweat when he lifted his arm to strike.

"I didn't," cried Jacques. "I didn't throw anything."

"Don't deny it, ship's boy. I'll just have to cuff you again for lying. The thing hit me . . . here between the shoulders . . . it was cold and wet."

The cuffing didn't hurt much. Jacques stood up to it all right. The sailor's feet thudded off in the luminous night and Jacques dropped down on his all-fours

and felt along the deck.   His hands closed on something cold and slippery—a flying fish!   It must have
leaped from the sea and struck the sailor full upon his
naked back.   Jacques crouched down on the deck clutching the fish and half laughing.

Picard, pacing along deck with Susanne in one arm
and his violin under the other, bent down.

"What is it, Jacques, old fellow?   Why, bless my
heart, the lad's caught a fish.   Well, Susanne was only
just asking me: 'Picard, what's for supper?'   And I
hadn't the heart to tell her rancid bacon, I really hadn't."

Jacques laughed outright then, and in no time at all
he was comfortably curled against a big coil of rope on
which Marie was sitting, her cape pushed off, her neck-
erchief gleaming in the moonlight, her arms bare and
cool below her short sleeves.   Susanne munched fish-
bones between the feet of Monsieur Bosset seated on a
convenient capstan, palms propped on his fat knees.
Picard leaned his back against the rail and lifted his
bow.

Picard used to play his violin on the Pont Neuf with
the cooks and coachmen and lackeys from every great
house in Paris crowding close to listen.   It seemed
strange he should be playing now far away upon the
ocean with only Marie and Monsieur Bosset and
Jacques to hear him.

Beyond Picard's shoulder the *Renown* rode the sea
just by the shining moon-stream.   It reminded Jacques
of a far white château beside a shining river.   The
skipper once, running the *Swallow* up the river Loire
with a load of anchovies from the north coast of Brit-

tany, had made occasion to take Jacques to pay a visit to
a kinsman of theirs who was a servant in a château of
the country. There had been a fine party going on at
the time in the great hall of the château, and their kinsman had let them look in upon it.

When Picard played "The Bridge of Avignon,"
Jacques could see again as plain as day all the ladies
and gentlemen dancing the minuet under the painted
ceilings and crystal chandeliers.

> The ladies dance like this,
> The ladies dance like this . . .

Jacques could see brocaded skirts all strewn with
many-colored flowers billowing and foaming as the
ladies curtsied low to the music. There was one tune that
made Jacques think, instead, of faggots blazing on the
hearth and of Aunt Gabrielle singing as she stirred the
soup pot. So strong a memory was in this old favorite
of Aunt Gabrielle's that Jacques could almost smell cabbage soup when Picard played it. Another made him
think of Mardi Gras and merrymakers in their masks
running and laughing in the streets.

The good French tunes that Picard played must
have made Monsieur Bosset homesick for, in a little
pause, he sighed and said:

"Why wasn't I contented as things were? A pret-
tier business a man couldn't wish for than a cozy inn in
a port town with people always coming and going. I
wonder now—whatever made me leave the Little
Sailor?"

Marie spoke up quickly. The New World was the

world of opportunity.   To be sure it was.   Look at
Monsieur d'Iberville and his brothers now.   Their
father, plain Charles Le Moyne, son of a humble inn-
keeper in Dieppe, had gone to Canada, as every soul
in Dieppe could tell you, and the king had made a
noble of him.   And look at his sons, the eldest a baron,
as the good God was her witness, and the rest cap-
tains and lieutenants and what-not, the last one of
them.

"Eh, now, do they have nobles in the New World,
then, and did the king really make an inn-keeper's son
one?" asked Monsieur Bosset suddenly quite cheerful
again.   "Are you sure the father was no more than an
inn-keeper, Marie?"

"I come from Dieppe," said Marie.   "I've seen the
very inn many and many a time."

"A noble," chuckled Monsieur Bosset.   "Well, well."

Jacques must have fallen asleep then, because the
next tunes didn't seem to be played on a violin at all.
They were love-songs, "My Sweet Annette" and
"Charming Gabrielle" and songs like that.   Jacques
seemed to be lying in his bed at home hearing men outside in the street singing about their sweethearts—
sailors, he thought, from some ship that day arrived in
port.

It seemed to him that he got up out of bed and ran
to open the casement.   A fine blue and gold carriage
came rolling past and all the sailors cheered.   There
was a fattish gentleman in the carriage tricked out in a
blue satin coat with laces cascading over his plump
hands.   One of the sailors called up to Jacques that

it was the Baron Bosset just returned from the New World where he had made his fortune.

Jacques was asleep and dreaming it all of course. When he waked up there was no music and the boards felt hard under him. He thought at first that the musician and the listeners, all but him, had gone below. Then he saw Marie and Picard leaning at the rail. Marie was saying:

"But, my poor Picard, I am married already. My husband is a soldier—one of those Monsieur d'Iberville left to defend the little settlement. It is to join him I am making this long journey. Should I have told you earlier? Ah, my friend . . . "

Picard slumped down against the rail the way Jacques had done when the sailor had hit him.

A wind rose one night and by the next afternoon was blowing a hurricane. The sea seemed to rise to the very clouds and then, falling back on the decks of the *Palm Tree,* to threaten each time to send her to the bottom. Even the sailors were frightened. The very sea-wolves declared there were no such winds off Newfoundland and began to pray to St. Christopher, the patron saint of mariners. Jacques himself clasped his medal with the pictured saint walking steadfastly through the wild waters and looked at it often as Aunt Gabrielle had said he should do if he would be kept safe from harm.

Barrels of drinking water were thrown overboard to lighten the ship, and there was even talk of sending everybody's trunks and chests after them. It seemed to Jacques that it would be very hard if his stout little chest which had survived more voyages than anybody had ever counted must now be fed to the ravenous waves together with all the fine clothes the king had given him.

After dark the wind and the sea roared louder than ever. And the blackness was split again and again with saw-edged lightning. One clap of thunder like the end of the world itself struck the *Palm Tree*. There was a breath of shivering green-lighted waiting. The passengers huddled between decks shivered and held their breaths. Above them through the dull roar of the storm, came a sickening crack.

"The mainmast, the mainmast!" a sailor shouted.

"Ah," moaned Monsieur Bosset wetting his lips. "Another blow like that will finish us. And to think I might this moment be sitting snug and dry in the kitchen of the Little Sailor."

Monsieur Bosset, however, was not destined to drown or Jacques to lose his chest. By morning they were running out of the storm. The sailors rigged up a jury mast with one of the spare spars which they carried lashed along the bulwark rail for just such emergencies. The only casualties were of the sheep and poultry which were found to have smothered shut up in the hold. They had to be flung overboard, and the *Palm Tree* went wallowing along through heavy seas.

The day they reached the tropic, Jacques was hauled out of his hammock when it was barely light to carry buckets to fill a huge iron-bound keg the sailors had set on the afterdeck. The crew was, of a sudden, in high good humor. They laughed and joked and made bets as to whether the ship's commander would let them

duck him in his fine lieutenant's uniform or get himself
off with a fine.   They chaffed every soul who came on
deck: "Are you ready now for your baptism, Monsieur,
or will you have your breakfast first?"

Jacques got well splashed trotting back and forth
with the buckets they kept hauling up over the ship's
side.   Indeed he got his baptism long before it came
his turn to be ducked.   But he took his ducking all
the same, the first of all, laughing and spluttering and
pretending to struggle with the four great hands that
thrust him in.   And, when the sailors dropped him on
deck again, he raised his hand and solemnly swore after
them that so long as he should follow the sea he would
let no man pass the tropic without the sacred ceremony.
Then he shook himself like a puppy, scattering drops
of water everywhere, and danced about the next vic-
tim—Monsieur Bosset it was, by chance.   Beads of
perspiration dewed Monsieur Bosset's lip.

"I will pay," shrilled Monsieur Bosset.   "It's only
a franc, isn't it?   I will gladly pay."

Toward afternoon when the fun had spent itself,
Picard hunted Jacques up.

"Jacques," he began and then stopped, red and uncomfortable.   Jacques couldn't imagine what was
wrong.   "They've drowned Susanne," blurted Picard
at last.

"Who did it?" asked Jacques after a little.

"I don't know.   I found her in the bottom of the
cask with a belaying pin tied to her neck.   You know,
old fellow, they're drinking a lot.   Their pockets are
jingling to-day with all the fines they've collected."

Picard sewed Susanne up in a piece of sail cloth, and he and Jacques gave her the burial of the sea. As Jacques turned back from the rail he saw the royal commissary's son watching him. There was a peculiar mocking look in the sharp little black eyes.

"It was you," said Jacques. "It wasn't the sailors. It was you that drowned Susanne."

The commissary's son laughed. Jacques leaped upon him. Up flew the deck, down sank the sky. The sun was a red ball just where the sea and the sky came together. It danced up and down before Jacques' eyes as he sprang on the commissary's son, and they went down together, and up and down again, rolling on the hard boards.

"Go it, ship's boy. Go it. Punch him once for me."

Sailors' faces shut out the dancing sun. The faces were red and hot. Jacques always had wanted to fight the commissary's son. But now he found he didn't like it after all. It was like hitting something soft and dead wrapped up in sail cloth.

"Aw, don't stop, ship's boy. Don't stop *now*. You've just got him where you want him."

But Jacques did stop. The commissary's son picked himself up weeping and ran off, calling his father. Jacques turned his back and walked away. All the sailors jeered.

Every soul aboard the *Palm Tree* was glad when at last, on an afternoon in late November, the look-out called "Land ho." Everybody ran on deck. The first of the West Indies Islands lay to starboard. A few hours later, they sighted the great rock sailors called the "Barn" because it rises so steeply from the sea. And finally as dark was falling they came under a promontory with a little town twinkling at the bottom and a fort cut into the rock to guard the harbor. The *Renown* fired her signal guns, was answered by the guns of the fort, and glided inside, followed by the brig. The *Palm Tree* limped in last of all and let down her ponderous anchors with a mighty clanking of chains.

CHAPTER VI

Salute of Seven Guns

Monsieur d'Iberville had the crews get the ships ready for sea again as fast as possible. They took on wood and water, replenished the spoiled stores, bought chickens and sugar, made biscuits, herded aboard twenty head of cows and beeves and three mares and a stallion and a great squealing drove of the wild island hogs. And then the ships stood out to sea once more.

The Gulf of Mexico is very blue, all roofed over with blue heavens where white clouds roll themselves up and glisten in the sun. Under the white clouds, white gulls swing. And in the water, round-backed porpoises hump themselves over and go down again like great wheels turning.

The ships from France sailed easily up the Gulf and on a sunshiny day in mid-December stopped before a little deep-water harbor with white shining beaches plumed in dark pine-trees. Here they were at last. The continent toward which they had so long been traveling lay before their eyes. A tiny new log fort with a dozen old cannon stood at one side of the harbor. It was Spain's feeble claim to a share in Monsieur d'Iberville's Gulf Coast empire. The paltry palisade was hardly breast high. A gunner aboard the *Palm Tree* declared it was more like a horse lot than a fort and boasted they could wreck it with one sharp broadside. He said the thing for Monsieur d'Iberville to do was to train his guns on the place right now and clear the Spaniards out once and for all. But Monsieur d'Iberville instead sent an officer in a small boat inside the harbor to get permission for his ships to enter, and the only guns fired were the guns of ceremony: seven in salute from the French ships, seven in polite response from the despised fort.

Some Spanish officers who came out to visit the French ships were able to give Monsieur d'Iberville news of his colony, which lay farther west along the seaboard. A boat from there had recently visited the Spanish post, had only just left, in fact, on its way to try to beg a little corn from the Indians near-by. The news from Monsieur d'Iberville's colony was not good. Many of the people were sick. Many had died, among them the commandant. Monsieur d'Iberville's young brother Bienville was acting commandant. The springs the people had got water from were dried up. The colony had had no flour for months now. The lard and wine were gone. The Spaniards themselves were hungry. You could tell by the way they pinched up crumbs off the cloth—Monsieur d'Iberville had invited them to stay for dinner on shipboard. But they liked telling Monsieur d'Iberville what a hard time his colony was having. And they watched him greedily while they told him.

Monsieur d'Iberville flushed and spun the stem of an emptied wine-glass between his blunt fingers. But he smiled all the same and said he had some news for the

Spaniards, too: he said he was come to the New World this time to move his settlement nearer to his Spanish friends. The place he described as "the river and bay above Massacre Island."

Then the Spanish officers squirmed and fingered *their* wine-glasses, but they went on pretending to be enjoying themselves. Monsieur d'Iberville signed to Jacques, the ship's boy, to fill the glasses. And in a minute they were all drinking reciprocal toasts: "Long live the king of Spain," from the French officers and "Long live the king of France," from the Spanish officers. And the Spanish lieutenant major added politely: "Long live Monsieur d'Iberville."

The next day Monsieur d'Iberville sent by land and sea to tell his colony of the proposed change of base. And eighty men were picked to ship for Massacre Island. The very name set Jacques' pulses throbbing every time he heard it. He wanted with all his heart to go along. Workmen of all sorts were the first chosen: wood-saw-yers, locksmiths, carpenters—Picard among others; then sailors from the crew, because they were strong and could help heave up logs. Then passengers, who were tired of being on shipboard and hated the idea of staying behind there in the Spanish harbor, waylaid the royal commissary as he went about the ships' decks making up the list, and declared they had an aptitude for building. Even Monsieur Bosset got himself taken on. The commissary's son was going. But Jacques remained unchosen. He thought of appealing to Monsieur d'Iberville, but Monsieur d'Iberville fell ill—so ill that he had to submit to an operation on shipboard.

After that the royal commissary was Jacques' only hope. That gentleman had a finger in every pie, from hiring a Spanish ketch for which its master asked seven francs a ton, to quarreling with the sailors over the exact quantity of building tools, cannon, foodstuffs, beads, blankets, and vermilion to be loaded on the little fleet of hired and borrowed boats. Everywhere you looked you saw Monsieur Nicolas' purple plume nodding emphatically and heard his pompous voice talking about the "king's money." You'd have thought he was no less than the king's minister to hear him roaring about the ships' decks. Jacques, much as he disliked the man, put himself in his path at every turn, running errands unasked and inventing ways to serve him. But it did no good. Monsieur Nicolas was too swollen with importance to notice a mere ship's boy.

However, on the day the boats were ready to leave for Massacre Island, Jacques swallowed his pride and openly accosted the commissary:

"If you please, Monsieur, I signed on for shore duty."

"You did, eh? What sort of shore duty?"

Jacques' ears got hot. He didn't know. He should have known of course. Hadn't he, the day they sailed from France, held in his own hand the detailed instructions from Versailles? But the sentence about his duties was precisely that which Jacques had skipped. Now all he could do was blush and stammer.

"Hm," said Monsieur Nicolas, "ever been apprenticed to any trade? No? Never been anything but a ship's boy? What's your name?"

"Jacques Duval, if you please, Monsieur."

The commissary thumbed the lists he carried until he came to Jacques' name and whatever it was that was written after it.

"Well," he decided, "I suppose you may as well serve as carpenter's helper as anything else while you're waiting for your real duties to begin.   Pack your kit-bag—"

"I have a chest, Monsieur."

The commissary smiled sourly.

"Your chest, then.   Put it aboard the ketch and lose no time about it.   And . . . " as Jacques was about to run . . . "understand, there's no extra pay in this."

Picard grasped Jacques' shoulder.

"What's he talking about?" whispered Picard. "What are these 'real duties' of yours which will begin later?"

"I don't know," Jacques owned, and, as soon as the commissary was out of hearing, "I had a chance to read all about it in Monsieur d'Iberville's sailing orders, but I was so excited I sort of skipped over that part.   But I don't see any use bothering about it, Picard.   I can do what any other boy could, I guess."

"Yes," agreed Picard, creasing his red cloth cap thoughtfully between his fingers.   "But, man or boy, it's only right a chap should know what it is he puts his name to."

Marie was one of those who had to stay behind on the French ships in the harbor of the Spaniards.   As Jacques was about to leave the *Palm Tree,* she came running up to say good-by.

"Jacques, will you do me a favor?"

A norther was blowing.   The tropical brilliance of

those first days in the Gulf was gone.   The sky and the
water were steely gray.   The wind came straight offshore.   It cut in through Jacques' good thick coat as if
it were no more than muslin.   Jacques shivered.

"Of course, Marie.   What is it?"

"If a soldier named Pierre Coudret is with the troops
ordered to meet you at Massacre Island, will you give
him a message?   Tell him—when no one is by listening—tell him Marie has come all the way from Dieppe,
and she is ready to forgive and forget if he is.   Remember, Jacques—if he is."

The corners of Marie's linen cap sticking out from
under her blue hood flapped about in the wind like
stricken gulls' wings.   Jacques saw them beating about
high over his head as the little ketch drew off from the
tall *Palm Tree*.   And then he lost sight of the white
fluttering bits altogether when the ketch leaned in the
wind and stood out to sea.

CHAPTER VII

MASSACRE ISLAND

MASSACRE ISLAND lies between the Gulf and a wide-mouthed bay. Usually it glitters like a hard bright jewel, its crystalline sands blindingly bright between a sea and sky of ineffable blue, its pines and Lebanon cedars distilling sweet steam into the hot sunshine. Jacques was to see it like that again and again. But that was not the way he saw it first, not at all.

From the Spanish fort to the island was a journey of only fourteen leagues. But in that north wind it had taken them the better part of two days to make it. And even arrived offshore, they were not able to enter the harbor, but had to lie to in the roads and unload as best they could in small boats. Jacques was in the first boat to go off.

Raked by the wind out of the north, the bare flat sands glimmered, bleak as a snow waste. The high-branching pine-trees afforded no shelter from the wind. Overhead the lofty boughs rocked and wailed. Underneath, the palmettos, torn to rags and beaten flat, whipped the ground without ceasing. The air was filled with white, stinging sand. It got in Jacques' nose and throat and choked him and stung his eyeballs so that tears ran down his cheeks.

They dumped the first boat-load of stores on the

beach. Two of the sailors rowed back for another load. Jacques stayed with the other two to move the boxes and bags beyond the tide line on the beach. When they had got everything moved, they set about to cover the heap with tarpaulin. That job was unbelievably hard. The whirling sand blinded them. Again and again a corner of canvas snapped out of hand at the moment of making it fast. The second boat and then the third was unloaded at the water's edge before they had got the first lot under cover.

The sailors sent Jacques to see if he could discover any sign of the boats from the colony ordered to meet them here. Jacques ran up the dune on the Gulf side and seeing nothing from there made his way along the beach toward the western end of the island. As he ran he stubbed his toe on something round and smooth and hard thrusting up from the sand. It seemed at first to be an overturned sea-shell, but when he stooped to pick it up he saw that it was a human skull. Other skulls lay farther along, and arm bones and thighs and ribs, all scoured clean by the harsh white sand—the bones of a hundred men or more. Scattered among them was a litter of broken bowls and pots for cooking. Some tribe from the mainland had been pursued here by their enemies and massacred—or so Monsieur d'Iberville had guessed upon a night last summer.

Just then out of the west between the line of islands and the coast appeared a sail and then another and another. Monsieur d'Iberville's brother Bienville was on his way to the rendezvous. Jacques turned and ran back along the beach, keeping close to the water where

the sand was packed as hard as a ship's deck.   The
wind took his breath; but when he came in sight of the
canvas-covered hummocks under the pine-trees and the
sailors laboring at them he managed to cry out:

"They're coming!   They're coming!"

Monsieur de Bienville's company landing at Massacre
Island were as brown, Jacques thought, as savages must
be.   They were thin, too.   Their sunburned skin hung
on their bones as loosely as their ragged clothes hung on
their backs.   But they were gay, laughing and joking
and flinging their arms about the shoulders of the new
arrivals.

Monsieur de Bienville himself was a surprise to
Jacques.   For some reason Jacques had expected him
to be tall and commanding like Monsieur d'Iberville.
But he was in fact nineteen years younger than his illus-
trious brother.   He was undersized, a slender stripling, barely twenty-one, with gentle soft lips almost like
a girl's, and eyes that seemed to be full of dreams.   He
wasn't nearly so impressive as Major Boisbriant, his
friend and commander of the troops.

The royal commissary came ashore from the sloops
while Monsieur de Bienville's party was landing.   He
evidently sized up Monsieur de Bienville as somebody
he needn't bother to respect, for when Monsieur de Bienville asked him to issue axes to the men so they could
get out saplings for tent poles before dark, the commissary merely shrugged his shoulders.

"I have no orders about furnishing tools to your
men," he said indifferently.   "If they haven't their own,
it's hardly my affair."

"THEY'RE COMING!"

Monsieur de Bienville looked surprised. He hesitated while he stared at the mean-visaged man in shabby court finery. The wind tore at the bedraggled purple plume on Monsieur Nicolas' rusty black hat. Monsieur de Bienville's lips parted in a soft smile.

"Perhaps you will sell me axes, Monsieur?" he asked. "Yes? Forty, if you please. The king is in my debt— twelve hundred francs, lieutenant's pay for the past year, you know. Just enter the axes on that account, if you please."

His friend Major Boisbriant smiled behind his hand at that. And Jacques grinned maliciously at the commissary's son. Monsieur Nicolas bit his lips and got red in the face. But he couldn't, of course, make further objection. And in a little while the lean Canadians were swinging bright new axes. The rhythmic blows had a hearty sound in the monotonous roar of the wind.

Jacques had Marie's message on his conscience. He inquired among the soldiers for Pierre Coudret. One of them pointed out a man with an enormous red beard who was just walking away from the rest with his ax on his shoulder. Jacques ran after him.

"If you please, Monsieur, I have a message for you—"

The red-bearded man turned and faced him.

"A message, eh? You've come on the ships from France, haven't you? Well, I don't care to hear anything you have to say. I came to the New World on purpose to put an ocean between me and the Old. I'll take it as a kindness if you'll keep your messages to yourself." He looked down at the sand while he was talking, but at the last he looked up and met Jacques' eyes squarely. "To yourself," he repeated. "I'll not have my affairs gossiped about."

And then for no apparent reason he swung his new ax down and lopped off a palmetto stalk. The fan-like leaves sped away rustling across the sands like the skirts of dancing ladies. Pierre Coudret watched them go. Then he shouldered his ax and continued his way leaving Jacques staring after him.

The Canadians under Major Boisbriant's command got the tents up on the lee side of the dune. They set up a canvas wind-break, too, and dug a pit and built in it a huge pine-log fire. While this was going on some of them took guns and went off down the island and shot shrill, gray-feathered bustards. When they came back they plucked the bustards and spitted them and roasted them odorously over the red logs. Oh, they knew a thing or two about making themselves and others comfortable, those Canadians of young Monsieur de Bienville.

After supper, as dark closed down, everybody drew in to the shelter of the canvas wind screen beside the fire and talked. The Canadians said the ships from France hadn't come a minute too soon. The colony had been living on corn for three months. And nobody had had a taste of wine for longer than that. Besides, they'd all like their last year's pay and clothes to cover their nakedness. They were glad to abandon the post where they had had such a hard time. They hoped things would go better at the new location. They weren't as eager as you'd have expected for news from France. Many of them were Canadians of course. But even to the native-born French France seemed to have become remote and unreal. But they were all full of questions about their Spanish rivals. So they were nearly naked now? And hungry, eh? Well, they'd give up before long surely. Then Monsieur d'Iberville could take the place over and build a proper French fort.

The newcomers, too, cheered by the sweet crisp bustard flesh and the fragrant pine blaze, loosed their tongues. Mostly they prattled of the dreams that had brought them to the New World: beaver skins and pearls and gold-mines. Monsieur Bosset tried to puzzle out where he should set his inn—whether on the mainland under the shelter of that fort Monsieur de Bienville was going upriver to build or here on the island near the king's storehouse.

"Well," somebody suggested, "here you'd catch the trade of ships when they came in port—"

"But Massacre Island," said Monsieur Bosset shivering slightly, "is not an inviting name, now, is it? Not a name to catch the timid souls at all."

Everybody laughed. And then the soldiers began to push and shove at Picard to make him play his violin. They crowded close around him like thirsty men pressing in to a tap. The thin sweet strains of music rose strangely up and up to where the moaning pine-trees rocked in the dark and broke there in a fine crystal shower like a tiny rocket. The frail aspiring sparks of sound shivered against the roaring dark and vanished.

Picard played "My Sweet Annette," and some of the

soldiers, each thinking no doubt of his own sweetheart, sang it with him softly.   Then he played "Pierre Bagnolet," that comic marching song of an army in flight from the enemy:

> Let us have legs
> Since he has arms!
> On your tiptoes,
> On your tiptoes!

Then he played the "Old Soldiers' Chorus."   They all knew that one and everybody sang lustily:

> They can talk about war
> Who have never been there,
> But I tell you, my friend,
> It's a sorry affair;
> And many a brave soldier,
> Many a comrade true,
> Therein has lost his life—
> And cap and jacket, too!

Jacques drew his blanket close around him and sat down beside Monsieur Bosset dozing now against a pine-tree.   Jacques shut his eyes.   He was very tired. But at first he was wide awake.   Against his close-shut eyelids pressed the sense of infinite inky seas tossing and heaving about a stark white island barren of any shelter or defense, on which the wind charged down like merciless armies.   He went to sleep at last, though, and dreamed about being in his own bed at home in a walled town where sailors, when they are in port, go singing through the quiet streets.

CHAPTER VIII

A Message on a Tree

JACQUES was almost sorry to leave Massacre Island. There had been no more wind after that first night, and he came near forgetting how dreary it had seemed on landing. After five days he remembered instead the way the cedars and pines smell under the sun; and how, on the Gulf side of the island, the waves flash up in air all spangled with the fish they carry as in an invisible net. He remembered the tug of a redfish on the end of his line and the taste of oysters when you have roasted them in their shells in good red embers.

The men were building a storehouse to guard the king's goods. And it was almost finished now. The walls made of pine-trees squared into logs and fitted one upon the other, were all up. The roof was the only thing lacking. Monsieur de Bienville detailed ten men to stay on the island under command of the royal commissary and cover the storehouse with a palmetto thatch. He and Major Boisbriant took everybody else with them to go and build the fort Monsieur d'Iberville had ordered.

Jacques wanted, of course, to go with Monsieur de Bienville and Major Boisbriant. He certainly didn't want to stay behind with Monsieur Nicolas. But all the same he felt a little sorry to see the shining island slip back and back and then lose itself altogether in the blue water.

They landed on the mainland and bivouacked on a curving beach all set about with live-oaks. The live-oaks had strange elfin branches with silky gray moss, so long it brushed the ground. Spanish beard, the soldiers called it, but Jacques thought it was more like French courtiers' wigs all curled and scented.

It was hardly the middle of January, but Jacques next morning found violets blooming at the feet of the be-wigged old oaks and a jasmin vine heavy with yellow aromatic bells. The jasmin was exactly like the plant the sailor had brought back last year for Jacques to set out in the walled garden. Jacques saw growing all about a shrub the Canadians said was called yaupon and was sacred to the Indians. It was a kind of smooth-leaved holly with coral-red berries thick-clustered on its silver stem. And he saw a cardinal flash like a flame through the gray tresses and dark green leaves of the oaks. So interested was Jacques in his discoveries through the woods alongshore that he wandered farther than he realized and came alone and unsuspecting on a little heap of embers on the beach with a thread of smoke breathing up from it.

Over the embers some pieces of meat were toasting on a rude wooden rack. A reed basket hung on a sweet myrtle bush. Jacques inspected its contents cautiously: several sorts of seeds in little skin pouches, each kind to itself; a small store of yaupon leaves; wool rolled into balls; mussel shells; small bones; roots that

looked like ginger; birds' claws; hoofs of some small
animal; feathers of red-birds and blue jays; a pair of
shoes curiously fashioned of skin as soft as chamois.
All about the fire the sand was scuffed and rumpled.   At
one side lay a broken earthen pot.   The pot was very
like those Jacques had seen on the island, among the lit-
tered skeletons of the massacred tribe.   He turned
and ran.

Near the place where they had slept, the young Bienville in his lieutenant's uniform was standing beside a
tree, cutting the bark away with his knife.   Jacques' face
must have been as white as the sand, for Monsieur de
Bienville, before Jacques spoke a single word, let fall
the hand with the knife in it and stared.

"Indians!" panted Jacques.   "Indians!   I am sure,
Monsieur.   I saw their campfire.   It is still smoking—
yonder past that little cape.   And they left a lot of
their things.   A broken pot is still wet inside."

Monsieur de Bienville smiled.

"Why not?" he said.   "They often come to the coast
for a bit of fish when they are tired of eating flesh."
He returned to his carving.   When he had cleared all
the bark away from a rough square, he took from his
pockets some ink and a little paint-brush.   "I am just
leaving a message for any who come along and see
where *we* have camped.   See?   Men with their arms
akimbo—they picture the French that way.   It is a pose
they never assume themselves.   A calumet—that is their
pipe of peace.   It will show that we are friendly.
Boats.   A log hut to say we're on our way to make
a settlement."

Jacques drew near and watched the singular message take shape under Monsieur de Bienville's hand. As he painted, Monsieur de Bienville talked. He talked about the savages. He said they were men after all, not wild beasts. It was a mistake to let oneself fear them. The Spanish did that and that made them cruel and harsh which in turn made the Indians fear the Spanish and hate them.

"We manage differently," said Monsieur de Bienville. "When we thread the swamps and rivers in our pirogues we go always laughing and singing."

A picture came into Jacques' mind of a tiny boatload of white men on a mysterious river, singing as they rowed. In the prow stood this young man with his girlish lips all gay and laughing. From the thick forests on the banks a host of naked savages peeped and listened.

"Even when we feel afraid in our hearts we never let them guess it. We are after all a mere handful. There are thousands upon thousands of them. And they are savages."

Monsieur de Bienville added a fringed palmetto thatch to the log hut he had just drawn.

"It is mere prudence to permit oneself no fear. Besides, you came here to be useful to the colony, did you not?" He plucked a bit of moss from the branches over his head to dry his brush on and looked at Jacques. Jacques wet his lips with his tongue, but no word came. "Your very first duty should be to get over feeling afraid of the natives of the country. Don't you think so?"

When Monsieur de Bienville smiled, he seemed hardly

more than a boy himself. He really wasn't a great deal taller than Jacques, who was tall for his age.

"Yes, Monsieur," breathed Jacques at last.

Monsieur de Bienville had brought along in his little fleet two Indian boats made of logs hollowed out by fire and then scraped with shell tools—pirogues they called them. One of the two was so vast that, if it hadn't been loaded with supplies, it could have carried sixty men, Picard said.

Jacques and Picard traveled by chance in the smaller of the two pirogues going up the bay. It was a fresh fair morning, a little cool but sun-drenched. The water danced and sparkled under the blackened snout of the pirogue. The sails the sloops carried puffed out like balloons. The heavily freighted fleet moved slowly past the beaches with their glossy-leaved magnolias and live-oaks where the long mosses blew, and came at last into a river delta with grass-lipped bayous and flat marshy islands. The islands were tawny like sleeping panthers. They were covered with dry, gold-colored reeds which quivered like hair in the light breeze.

The Canadians said the reason Monsieur d'Iberville was going to set his colony on this river instead of on the Mississippi was that higher up there were some good, high bluffs to build on. And, besides, the country this river ran through had more Indians living in it.

Picard carried his violin. He was never separated from it, indeed. The soldiers had dubbed it "Madame" as though it were Picard's wife.

"Let's sing," cried Jacques.

The sails of the officers' boat curtsied a moment before it passed the pirogue.   If the young lieutenant standing in the bows talking with his friend the major looked by any chance toward the pirogue, he saw Picard fiddling gaily, the two Canadian soldiers singing as they rowed, and Jacques standing up singing and smiling.

The little pirogue lagging behind slid its bows close under the shadow of tall reeds.   Jacques heard a faint rustling.   It was a mere whisper—he hardly heard it above their song and the lapping of the oars.   As the pirogue nosed into sunshine again the gold reeds back of it parted like a curtain.   A man stood up full height. He was naked and his dark body was painted all over in many colors.   He wore on his brow a turkey's skin. The turkey head seemed to be stuffed.   The beak thrust forward over the man's face and the feathered skin rippled back and down over his ears.

The song dried on Jacques' lips.

"Look," he gasped.   "Look . . . no, not there, *back* of us."

But by the time Picard and the Canadians looked where Jacques pointed, there was nothing to be seen but the plumy sedge shaking and rustling as though a quick gust of wind had passed along it.

CHAPTER IX

The Iron Hand

THE second morning they drew in before a high steep bluff of red and parti-colored clay: "the second bluff on the left, sixteen leagues above Massacre Island," it was described in Monsieur d'Iberville's dispatches. Across the river the buttressed, mammoth cypresses rose out of wide lakes milky white under an early morning mist. The leafless branches towered to incredible heights. So big appeared the cypresses in the opposite swamp and so many, too, that if everyone could be fashioned into a pirogue, Picard said, there would be room in that fleet for all the people in France.

Monsieur Bosset, too, waxed eloquent at the Promised Land, now they had really got to it. He declared the river more considerable than the Seine before Rouen. And in the first minute after he had scrambled panting to the top of the bluff, he discovered a mulberry-tree for all the world like the mulberries of Provence.

"And the climate is the same. I do declare it is. The air has the very same softness against the cheek." He went running about with the mulberry twig in his hand, showing it to everybody. "See, Monsieur? It is mulberry, on my soul. All we need now is silk-worms, and the ladies of our colony can go dressed in silks, eh,

Monsieur? Jacques, my boy, you must put that news in the letter you have promised to write to Madame for me. It will cheer the good soul to hear about the silk dresses she can wear when she comes to the New World."

They planted in the ground a cross with the arms of France painted on it. And at Monsieur de Bienville's command the soldiers fired off their muskets three times. Each time everybody cried, "Long live the king!" Then Monsieur de Bienville read from a paper a long proclamation beginning: "In the name of the most high, mighty, and invincible Prince, Louis the Great, by the grace of God King of France and of Navarre, Fourteenth of that name, I take possession of this river and bay and all the lands they water . . ." Then one of the priests said a prayer beside the cross and everybody knelt down around it and sang a churchly chant.

Jacques felt that somebody was watching them. He stole a glance over his shoulder. A little way off through the thick trees stood three naked men with copper-colored skin and bright feathers in their hair. One of the Canadians discovered the savages at the same moment Jacques did and touched Monsieur de Bienville's arm. Monsieur de Bienville got to his feet and beckoned the savages to come nearer. He sent some of the soldiers to unload the boats in a hurry so they could get out some beads and things.

The savages greeted Monsieur de Bienville by rubbing their hands over his breast and stomach and then over their own. Then they went up to the wooden cross and rubbed it and then rubbed themselves. Maybe they thought it was some kind of French god because they had seen everybody kneeling around it. One of them took a calumet out of a skin pouch slung at his shoulder. The long stem had a floating fan of white swan feathers hanging down from it—for peace and friendship, one of the Canadians whispered to Jacques. If it had been a war-pipe it would have had flamingo feathers the color of blood.

The man with the calumet took tobacco out of a little bag. But before he filled the big pipe-bowl he flung a bit of the tobacco at the wooden cross. He got fire with two bits of wood and a scrap of dry moss in his palm. The first puff of smoke he blew to the sky, the second toward the cross, and then he blew one to each of the four winds. And after that he handed the pipe to Monsieur de Bienville who took great care to smoke it in exactly the same way before he passed it on to Major Boisbriant.

When all the officers had smoked, presents were given to the savages: beads and bells and mirrors and vermilion. The savages thanked Monsieur de Bienville by rising and crying *hou, hou, hou* three times and elevating their hands. Their gibberish sounded to Jacques like his African parrot's talk. One of them kept grunting to himself, and that sounded like the wild island hogs the Canadians were this minute bringing ashore from the boats. The savages didn't sound a bit like real people talking. And when at last they went away through the trees their feet made no more noise than dry leaves make in falling.

From that very first day everybody was busy. The

men cut down the trees: red and white oaks, laurel, sassafras, mulberry, sycamore, walnut, and towering pine. Some they squared into logs to build the fort with. They dug a powder pit at the edge of the bluff and set up on scantlings the skeleton of a big flat-boat to do ferriage duty later on between the settlement and Massacre Island. It would be weeks before Monsieur d'Iberville could get well enough to come climbing up the red clay bluff and write down the record of these accomplishments in the journal he kept day by day for the king to read in his far-off painted palace. Meantime everybody worked. And while the work went on, spring, which came so early hereabout, stole on. Partridges whistled in the edge of the clearing, and the huckleberry flushed and then whitened. Over the river against the dim gray tangle of branches and moss, the rare swamp maple flamed alight.

Soon Jacques was wakened every morning by wild turkey cocks saluting each other from the sun-brightened tops of the cypresses on the swamp. On those level greening treetops as in an aerial meadow they called the tidings of dawn exactly as the cocks crow in a French back-yard. One took it up from another and then another until the high forests rang with their jubilation and the whole world seemed to shout.

From the minute Jacques, in the tent where he slept, drew on his shoes at sunrise he was kept busy running errands. He trotted about all day waiting on the workers, fetching their tools and tobacco and drinking-water and, at meal-times, their bowls of steaming saga-

mité, that mush the savages had taught them to make
of the native corn.

Now and then more savage visitors came on quiet
feet out of the woods around the clearing, their feather
head-dresses flaming suddenly out of the shadows, bright
as the maple in the swamp across the river, or the red-
bird that came every day to perch on the new flagpole.
They usually came to bring something as a gift for
Monsieur de Bienville or to offer in trade at the king's
warehouse: a deerskin dressed and painted with curious
pictures, or some smoked venison, or a skin full of their
much-prized bear oil—"a deer of oil" the Canadians
called it, giving it an exact value in trade like a yard of
French cloth or a pair of shoes. Jacques got so he
wasn't the least bit afraid when an Indian appeared abruptly in the clearing. He asked Picard if he was.

"Well," said Picard, "smoking the peace-pipe and
swapping presents here at the white men's fort isn't the
whole story, you know. I'm not sure I'd like to meet
a party of them off by myself hunting in the woods."

Monsieur Bosset got lost. He wandered impru-
dently into the forest surrounding the half-built fort and
did not come back. Every morning they fired the cannon to guide him home. And squad after squad of
searchers combed the woods for him. Pessimists pre-
dicted he'd never be heard from again. He might have
run upon a rattlesnake. And there were other dangers
in these woods besides rattlesnakes, the good God knew.
The savages were at war among themselves. Their
blood-red arrows were whistling on every wind up-

country now.   It was no place for a Christian, least
of all the soft, helpless little inn-keeper.

The Canadians talking about the supper fires told
the newcomers all they knew about Indians.   Jacques
heard of the Black Drink, made of the sacred yaupon
leaves, of scalping, of burnings alive, of one wretch made
to hold his fingertips down in his captors' pipe-bowls
while they went on smoking.

The third day after Monsieur Bosset got lost, there
came to the new fort a firm-jawed man whose right hand
had been shot away at the wrist.   He had replaced it by
an iron hook with which deftly he served himself
whether he wanted to draw his canoe inshore by a wide-
rooted cypress or merely to turn the pages of the latest
dispatch from Monsieur d'Iberville.   His real name
was Henri de Tonti, but everybody called him by a
name the Indians had given him—the Iron Hand.

Years ago in company with La Salle, the Iron Hand
had set out from Canada and explored the unknown
Mississippi all the way to the Gulf, planning a great
Gulf Coast empire firmly banded to Canada by the
broad Mississippi valley.   To that end the Iron Hand
had built a tiny fort mid-continent and waited while La
Salle was fetching colonists from France.   La Salle,
as everyone knows, returning through the Gulf of Mexico, missed altogether the mouth of the Mississippi and
landed his ill-starred boatloads farther to the west where
in time most of them died and La Salle's own blood was
wasted on the sand.   The Iron Hand meantime had left
his post and journeyed again down the winding river
to meet his friend, and not finding him had left a letter

for him in a tree, as one might drop a card upon a salver
—a letter which Monsieur d'Iberville's party, going up
the Mississippi fourteen years later, had bought from the
Indians at the price of an ax.   All the years between,
the Iron Hand had been at his lonely post in the middle
of the wide dark continent, waiting for France to make
the dream empire on the Gulf come true.   And now
having traveled by tedious pirogue down the Mississippi
once more, around the coast and up, here he was offering
his services at the new fort.

When the Iron Hand moved across the parade
ground in his suit of dressed deerskins, padding along
softly, but powerfully, too, with his woodsman's stride,
Jacques' eyes followed him thirstily as though he were a
god come down to earth.   Jacques was privileged one
evening to set before his hero a bowl of sagamité.   The
Iron Hand was talking to Monsieur de Bienville at the
time.   He did not look up from the rude map which
lay in the candle-light between them together with some
dispatches from Monsieur d'Iberville.   The big iron
hook shot out easily, encircled the hot bowl, and drew
it closer on the hewn-pine table.

"If you do go up-country," said Monsieur de Bienville, "where the Indian war is, you will of course need
an escort, as my brother Iberville suggests.   How many
men should you require?"

"Oh—six or eight," said the Iron Hand carelessly as
though it were a matter of no consequence whatever.

A film came over Jacques' eyes, and his throat felt
as if it had a string drawn around it.   Monsieur de
Tonti was a brave man, he thought as he crossed the

parade ground in the dark.   At the edge of the bluff
he stopped and watched a moon as red as Indian war-
paint rise above the flat-topped cypresses over the river.
The night was filled with the bellowing of alligators.

Jacques felt lonely.   He thrust his hand into his
jacket pocket and his fingers closed on something cool
and hard.   The saint whose image Aunt Gabrielle had
given him would always be standing at the throne of
heaven, she had promised, ready to pray for Jacques
when he needed it.   But none of the prayers Jacques
had learned from the priests fitted the present, somehow.   They belonged in a carved stone church with
candle-light and incense and music floating above the
bowed heads of women in caps all just alike, each with
two starched flaps white and pointed like angels' wings.
Here in the wild and lonely dark Jacques needed a new
prayer.

"Blessed Christopher, little silver saint," he prayed,
"ask the good God not to let the Indians hurt Monsieur
Bosset.   And make me brave like the Iron Hand.
Amen."

CHAPTER X

THE GRAVE IN THE WOOD

THE days went by and still Monsieur Bosset did not
come back. The Iron Hand set off on his mission up-
country. Monsieur d'Iberville, recovered at last,
brought the *Renown* and the *Palm Tree* to anchor at
Massacre Island and himself came sailing a shallop up
the river to the red clay bluff. He brought Marie and
all the others who had been left behind. From Massacre Island the royal commissary, Monsieur Nicolas,
came along, too, bringing his family. Madame, the
commissary's wife, declared in her high complaining
voice that sagamité was no fit dish for a lady—in France
one fed corn to fowls, not people. She pouted her lips
with the tiny dot of black court plaster just at one side
and said she'd rather starve than eat such savage messes.
The commissary's son made a sling and stole about the
edges of the clearing potting the mocking-birds and
cardinals in full song. And the commissary himself
tapped the ground with his ribboned cane and hinted
right and left that Monsieur d'Iberville's stripling
brother Bienville had plainly been wasting the king's
goods. He went about saying that the brothers were
thieves and rogues, both of them, and if they weren't
careful some honest man would certainly denounce them
to the king.

Jacques was very glad of course to see Marie again. But Marie seemed changed.   She inquired at once for the man called Pierre Coudret.   And when she learned that he was one of those who had gone with the Iron Hand up where the Indians were fighting, a blank, empty look came in her eyes.   She made Jacques repeat to her over and over, word for word, what Pierre Coudret had said to him at Massacre Island.   Every time Jacques came to the part about Pierre Coudret's having come to the New World on purpose to put an ocean between himself and the Old, tears ran down Marie's cheeks.   And she and Picard did not seem to be friends any longer—the way they used to be on shipboard. Marie in her familiar blue hooded cape was always wandering alone on the bluff watching for pirogues coming down the river.   And if she so much as met Picard on the parade ground or passed by the guard-house where he was laying split pine shingles on the scaffolding, she just looked the other way.   When Jacques asked Picard why that was, Picard said Marie was not to blame, because "a good woman has room in her heart for but one man."

Monsieur de Bienville told off a squad to carry food and instructions down to the detachment of soldiers who were staying on at the abandoned settlement on the Gulf Coast to destroy the fort there.   Picard, being young and restless, applied for permission to go along. Monsieur de Bienville consented at once.   Moreover he suggested that they take Jacques.

"It will be good experience for you," Monsieur de Bienville said smiling at Jacques.   "You will learn how

to get about in the forest.   And that will be of use to
you later on."

"Now what does he mean by that?" whispered Picard.

Jacques shook his head.   He didn't know any better
than Picard what Monsieur de Bienville meant, but all
the same he didn't want Monsieur de Bienville interrupted now: Monsieur de Bienville, as he talked, was
writing out an order to the royal commissary to let
Jacques have a gun.   Jacques had wanted a gun ever
since he could remember.   And the order called for
powder and shot besides.

Jacques saw the commissary's son eyeing him envi-
ously when he presented his order at the new-built warehouse.

"When are you going?" asked the commissary's son,
pressing close to look at the gun.

"To-morrow," said Jacques briefly, and walked away
with his gun at his shoulder.

He went out to the edge of the clearing where Picard
and another carpenter were shaping a forest pine-tree
into a ship's mast.   Jacques sat down on a stump with
his new gun on his knees and watched the two carpenters working.   The air was warm all around him,
and the freshly skinned pine shaft smelled sweet under
the sun.   The planes nibbled at each little roughness
with a hungry chewing sound, and the men's voices
mixed together in mild chat.   They talked about the
mast they were making and said that, when it was
finished, it would still have to be towed down to Massacre Island where the *Palm Tree* and the *Renown* were
now in harbor.   They approved their handiwork,

thought the *Palm Tree* would have a likelier mainmast than the one she had lost at sea—so long ago that seemed when you stopped to think. They speculated as to when the ships would sail back to France. They said Monsieur d'Iberville was just waiting for the Iron Hand to get back to the fort. Picard looked up and smiled and nodded at Jacques.

"They'll probably be gone by the time we come back from the Gulf Coast, eh, old fellow?"

Picard's saying that sent a shock of dismay through Jacques. Jacques had always known the *Renown* and the *Palm Tree* would sail back to France some day of course, known somehow that he was of those expected to stay behind in the new colony, but—

"That's a fine gun the boy has," said Picard's companion.

"It is that," agreed Picard heartily. "Jacques, suppose we try our hand at a bit of shooting when I get through here—just for practice. What do you say?"

Jacques smiled quickly.

"I'd like that," he said.

The mast was done by noon. Picard and Jacques set off through the woods north of the settlement. They walked some miles, and Jacques got a lot of practice in loading and firing. But they didn't kill anything.

The dogwood was in bloom. It lay about them shining against the night of the forest like stars in the sky. In the depths of the shadows they came suddenly upon a pit that was, strangely enough, the exact size and shape of a Christian grave. Heaped beside it was the fresh-dug brown earth, and, at one end, un-

believably and yet certainly, was a Christian cross made
of two sticks tied together with a bit of rag.

The silk rag tied around the crossed sticks looked
familiar somehow.   Jacques knelt down on the ground
to examine it more closely.   Picard gave a cry and
leaped the pit at one bound.   He ran to the blossoming dogwood tree just beyond.   A black heap huddled
at the tree-roots stirred and moaned.   Monsieur Bosset!   The poor little inn-keeper in the extremity of
despair had dug his own grave.   No wonder Jacques
had recognized the scrap of silk.   But the silk rag
looked more like Monsieur Bosset's good French neck-
erchief than the creature huddled under the black cape
looked like the round and bustling inn-keeper.

Fifteen days he had been without food or water.   He
could scarcely move with the two of them to support
him.   And he was quite out of his mind.   All the toil-
some miles back to the fort he was raving.   He fancied
himself in France again at the Little Sailor.   He was
ordering Madame, his wife, and the kitchen maid to
prepare a dinner for some traveling lord or other who
was just returned from the New World.

"Duckling, duckling, I said.   To be sure he wants
duckling.   And see to it you cook it properly.   Oh,
why is it, nobody outside of Rouen ever learns the secret
of cooking duckling?   These barons are not to be
trifled with.   That fowl must be toasted brown and
crackly on the outside and full of sweet juices within.
And good white bread.   And salad—crisp and piquant
—um—"   Saliva drooled down poor Monsieur Bosset's trembling chin and tears coursed over his flabby

cheeks. "Wine? Oh, yes, yes, yes. Moselle, cold, cold—good, cold Moselle."

On and on he gibbered, serving up his fancied dainties all the way home, and after they got him to bed, though his poor starved stomach couldn't retain so much as a spoonful of sagamité when they brought it to him.

When the commissary opened the king's warehouse next morning, Jacques was waiting outside. Jacques followed Monsieur Nicolas in and for two sous bought enough paper to write a letter on. As he ran off with the paper in his hand Jacques thought how Aunt Gabrielle would get the priest to read his letter to her and the skipper in the dark-beamed kitchen while the soup bubbled over the faggots—or, no, it would be summer of course, by the time the letter got to France, and they would sit in the walled garden. When he got back to the tent where he and Picard slept, Jacques sat down on a stool and spread the clean writing-paper carefully on top of his chest. Then he wrote:

MY DEAR FATHER AND AUNT:— We have built the fort.   It is named Fort Louis for the king. It has four bastions with six cannon at each corner and, inside of it, a parade ground and four buildings and a flagpole. We have started the barracks, too, and just above the fort Monsieur d'Iberville has laid out with pegs and strings the town lots where the colonists and priests will have their houses. We dug a powder-pit, too, but it got full of rain-water and that ruined it. And we are building a big flat-boat. My shirts are getting pretty

JACQUES KNELT DOWN TO EXAMINE IT MORE CLOSELY.

ragged from the briars. And my cap got burned up night before last from being left too close to the camp-fire to dry. My jacket got a little burned, too, at one of the pockets. I found my little St. Christopher in the ashes. It had rolled off. So it wasn't melted. Wasn't that lucky? Some people don't like sagamité, especially women. It is corn pounded up and boiled in water and seasoned with bear's grease. You eat it instead of bread. You take a bite of sagamité and then a bite of meat. There are a great many flowers in the woods now and berries of different kinds, but I don't know the names of them all yet. And there is a red-bird that sings on our flagpole. His song is so sharp it is nearly like a whistle. Monsieur Bosset got lost in the woods, but we found him. He was out of his head from starving so long and he couldn't eat. But he will soon get fat again, I guess. Some soldiers are going down on the Gulf Coast. Monsieur de Bienville said I could go, too. I am going now. Good-bye.

Your loving son and nephew,

JACQUES DUVAL.

P.S. I have a new gun, but I can't shoot it very well yet.

Picard came in just as Jacques got through writing his letter. He said Jacques would have to hurry, because the soldiers had finished loading the pirogues with the supplies they were to take down on the Gulf

Coast, and they were ready to start now. Picard helped Jacques seal up his letter with a generous blob of red sealing wax. Then Picard took up Madame, his violin, and Jacques got his gun and the new deerskin cap Marie had made to take the place of his French cap that had got burned up, and they left the tent. At the gate to the fort, Picard waited while Jacques ran inside to drop his letter in the letter-box at the king's warehouse. And then they scrambled down the bluff to the waiting canoes.

CHAPTER XI

Under the Flowered Flag

Coming upriver some two weeks after they had gone
down they met a shallop towing the mast for the *Palm
Tree* out through the sedgy islands.   They hailed her
to get the news.   Monsieur d'Iberville had not yet
started for France after all.   But he would have to wait
no longer now.   Advance messengers had arrived at
the fort with the news that the Iron Hand accompanied
by the chiefs of the warring nations would arrive at
Fort Louis in a few hours.   He was probably there
by now.   If so there would be great goings-on at the
fort to-day.

Moored in the river under the red clay bluff when
the returned travelers reached it lay a little fleet of
pirogues and canoes.   The unfinished flat-boat on its

scaffolding was empty of workmen. Atop the bluff quiet prevailed. Not a hammer or ax chopped into the solemn hush. There wasn't a soul in sight. The new log houses, some with palmetto thatch, some with no roof at all as yet, gave off a piney smell under the high sun. Through the open gate of the fort came the sound of a man's voice not in the everyday ease of conversation and not sharp and quick like the voice of an officer drilling troops, but sonorous and slow—in the tone of somebody making a speech. It was a speech in a savage tongue. Jacques couldn't understand a word, but it sounded impressive for all that. The new arrivals quenched the boisterous hails of greeting that trembled in their throats and slipped unobtrusively in through the gate.

On the parade ground between the government house and the king's magazine, all the colony was gathered. In the center on skins and mats spread on the ground sat the chiefs of the warring tribes and the Iron Hand and the brothers d'Iberville and de Bienville. Everybody else was standing close about solemn and intent. It was a motley crowd—bronzed and ragged Canadian wood-rangers; French soldiers and sailors, trim officers with gold braid and buttons flashing; naked Indians bright-crested as parrakeets; two priests in black robes; Marie in gray homespun with starched white linen kerchief and cap; the royal commissary carrying his ribboned cane and wearing a dingy court costume of mulberry satin topped off with an enormous curled wig and the hat with the bedraggled ostrich plume; his lady tricked out in rose brocade with gold threads a-shimmer,

pointing an applegreen parasol into the sun; Monsieur
Bosset almost plump again in his buttoned coat and
neat knee-breeches.   Over them all in the corner near-
est the river flew the lilied flag of France from the
peeled and polished shaft of a tapering forest pine-tree.

The presents that were to be divided among the
Indians were spread out temptingly on the ground between them—a great heap of powder and balls and bird-
shot and guns and hatchets together with copper cal-
drons glowing in the sun, and colored beads and a
hundred other glittering trifles.

The Iron Hand had taught some French to an Indian who had been serving him as a guide.   He himself knew more than one Indian dialect.   Monsieur
de Bienville had picked up an understanding of the
inter-tribal language in use all through the southern
country.   Sometimes one of them would interpret.
Sometimes another.

"Tell them," said Monsieur d'Iberville looking
toward the interpreters, "if they want our friendship
they must give their skins in trade to us, not to our
rivals."

The Indian chiefs listened respectfully as this was
translated to them.   Then a warrior rose, and, nodding
his plumed crest, made a long speech in his own tongue.
A warrior in the opposite party made a speech.

"Tell them," said Monsieur d'Iberville next, "there
must be no more bloodshed among themselves."

It was to Jacques a tedious ceremony—so many sonorous orations in a meaningless language, such tiresome
repetition by the interpreters, such long pauses while

the calumet with its floating swan feather fan passed
from hand to hand, and the slow spiral of peacemaking
smoke climbed from each successive mouth up into the
hot sun.   The calumet was returned to its dressed skin
bag at last and laid down carefully on the rack of two
forked sticks.   Then the chiefs rubbed white clay on
the faces of Messieurs d'Iberville and de Bienville.
Then one of them took Monsieur de Bienville on his
shoulders and leaped about with him while the others
beat time with their rattles made of dried gourds filled
with pebbles and whirled about on the ends of sticks—
chichicois, the rattles were called.

Jacques by chance held a chichicois in his own hand.
He had picked it up near a deserted Indian camp on the
coast.   He saw the commissary's son regarding it cov-
etously across the parade ground.   Jacques longed to
whirl it aloft and beat time with it as the Indians were
doing.   He believed he could.   He had practiced in
the pirogue all during the homeward journey on purpose to tease the commissary's son.   His hand moved
mischievously, and the pebbles in his gourd went clickety-
click.

"Tell them," said Monsieur d'Iberville, "the king
has sent a young French boy all the way across the ocean
to live with them and learn their language."

Jacques started.   All the eyes in the enclosure turned
his way.   Marie's, so blue under her starched white
cap, looked frightened.   Picard, close beside Jacques,
tried to smile at him, but he didn't succeed very well.
Monsieur Bosset pressed a white handkerchief against
his mouth and seemed to shake all over.   Even the com-

missary's son was startled.   He had just been taking
aim with his sling at the top of the flagpole.   His hands
fell back to his sides and he stared at Jacques.

Live with the Indians and learn their language.   The
words did not so much echo in Jacques' ears as they
wavered visionlike before his eyes, all graceful loops
and flourishes, shaped, to be sure, by a hand in a blue cuff
with lace on it.   That, certainly, was what had been
written in Monsieur d'Iberville's sailing orders and
Jacques had at the time neglected to read.   He could
almost see the unread sentence midway on the page
and he squinted up his eyes in a belated effort to spell
it out word by word.

The young Bienville moved from his place and
searched the crowd with his eyes.

"Does anybody know whether the boy Jacques Duval
—oh, there you are."   The lips that were nearly like
a girl's smiled as Monsieur de Bienville came toward
Jacques.   "Well, you just got back in time for your
great adventure.   What about it—are you ready?"

The Iron Hand turned around just then and looked
at Jacques for the first time.   Maybe Jacques only
imagined it, but it seemed—it really did—as if the
Iron Hand were taking his measure.

High at the top of the flagpole above the flowered
flag drooping like any old meaningless rag in the quiet
air, a cardinal perched, a drop of blood on the colorless
noon sky.   He sang his few clear notes, so achingly
sweet, and flew away.

Jacques drew a deep breath.

"Yes, Monsieur.   I am ready."

Marie went with Jacques to his tent to get his things together. It would be a long journey and only the first lap of it in pirogues. He couldn't take his chest of course, traveling such a long way afoot. Marie got her own flower-sprigged kerchief to pack his things in. Jacques took his clothes out of his chest and handed them to Marie piece by piece. She smoothed out the shirts and folded them carefully and rolled the stockings into tight hard balls. When the chest was empty, Jacques shut it up and sat down on it holding on his palm the medal Aunt Gabrielle had given him. The silver saint had on a tunic and he carried a tall staff to steady himself in the rough water. Around the picture of the saint with the boy on his shoulder was an inscription. It said: "Whosoever shall look upon the image of St. Christopher, on that day shall he neither faint nor fail."

Marie held out her hand.

"It will be safer in the bundle than in your pocket," she said.

So Jacques handed her the medal, too, and she laid it between the rolled stockings. And then she caught the corners of the kerchief together, two at a time, and tied them into firm knots. Then they went back across the open space grandly named Place Royale on Monsieur d'Iberville's map and into the log fort again.

The parade ground was in confusion now. The Indians were packing up their presents and getting ready to go. Monsieur de Bienville called Jacques to him and instructed him fully as to what was expected of him. He was to learn the Indian language, as stated—a charge plain enough in itself. But Jacques couldn't guess at all how the thing was to be done. How would he, to begin with, ever find out what all their gibberish *meant?* It would take, Monsieur de Bienville thought, two or three years for Jacques to learn all he should.

"For," he said, "it won't be enough just to pick up their words. You must watch everything they do and try to find out all you can about them—even what they think about."

Jacques kept his eyes fixed on Monsieur de Bienville's face. He listened carefully to every word that Monsieur de Bienville was saying. Monsieur d'Iberville all the while was telling the Indians, through the interpreters, that they were responsible for this boy's life:

"If the boy should be killed they will have to answer to us with their own blood."

Jacques couldn't help hearing what Monsieur d'Iberville was saying.

Every time Monsieur de Bienville so much as paused for breath, Monsieur Bosset would press close to Jacques and silently wring his hand as though there was small chance of their ever meeting again. Or Picard would whisper in Jacques' ear some bit of nonsense to help him keep his courage up and make him smile. And all the time Marie's blue eyes, staring at Jacques across his bundle tied up in her flower-sprigged kerchief, were shiny with tears.

All the colony pressed out to the edge of the bluff to see Jacques go away with the Indians. Looking up from a little pirogue, Jacques was reminded of the day the *Palm Tree* had sailed away from a crowded wharf in France. It was just as well, perhaps, that his father and his Aunt Gabrielle were not up there with his friends on the red bluff. It was hard enough as it was to go on smiling and waving to the end.

After the bend of the river hid the bluff and the fort and all his friends, Jacques could still hear the voices cheering and calling their good-byes after him. But beyond the second bend, he couldn't hear them any more.

CHAPTER XII

SECRET VILLAGES

THE noon sun beat straight down on the bright river. The naked Indian who faced Jacques in the pirogue wore bracelets that fell apart and then clinked together as he scooped up the river water on his paddle. He had great round patches of vermilion smeared about his eyes and a black half-moon painted on each cheek. A big pearl hung at his nose. His ears had been cut and stretched and wired so that they stood out from his head in great hoops that trembled when he moved. From his top-knot rose three swaying cock feathers. One was red, one yellow, one black.

In the bottom of the boat lay Jacques' gun and his bundle tied up in Marie's kerchief. He held in his hand the chichicois he had brought back to tease the commissary's son with. He must have been clutching it fast all this time without knowing it. Well—he tried to smile—he wouldn't need it now. An Indian rattle wouldn't be such a novelty where he was going.

He opened his hand over the edge of the boat and let the rattle fall into the river. The Indian brave watched him with expressionless eyes deep-sunk in those strange vermilion lakes painted on his face.

On the muddy banks of the river, alligators lay half-

buried.   They were ugly as toads and rough, like logs
with bark on them.   Sometimes they lay so still you
thought they were logs.   Sometimes they swam alongside the canoes, opening and shutting their jaws, and the
Indians would hit at them with their dripping paddles.
Once the boats passed a wide lagoon filled with lemon-
colored lilies as far as you could see.   The sun tilted
over at last and dropped behind the thick trees.   One
after another the canoes drew in beside a low bank
shaded by a grove of magnolias.   The boat Jacques sat
in nosed in among the rest.   The oarsman shipped his
paddles and signed to Jacques to get out.

Jacques picked up his gun and his bundle and stepped
out of the pirogue.   A path mounted the low bank
slantwise.   Jacques wondered how there came to be
a path in so wild and desolate a spot.   And then, as he
walked slowly up the path, he saw that it had not been
trodden by men's feet at all, but had been made by the
alligators.   The imprint of their scaly bodies against the
moist clay was quite plain.

The magnolias were in full bloom.   The blossoms,
big as people's faces, the color of cream, filled the air
with heavy perfume.   After the heat and glare of those
hours on the river Jacques felt all at once faint and ill
when he stepped into the chill sweet-smelling shade of
the magnolias.

The Indians wore at their belts little skin pouches
filled with reddish meal.   They dipped up water out
of the river in gourd cups, and each one shook into the
water a sparing quantity of his meal and drank the mix-
ture.   That was all the supper they had.   Several of

them offered their gourds to Jacques, but he didn't feel as if he could swallow a mouthful of that raw, cold mush. So he shook his head.

He stepped a little apart where the shade was deepest and stood clutching his gun and bundle. The savages seemed to be paying no attention to him. With their gourd cups they passed up and down the path to the edge of the water; or they lay under the magnolias with their pipes puffing slow smoke into the twilight.

One of them fashioned a kind of reed harpoon and tied it to his wrist with a cord of twisted bark. Then he sprang down the bank into one of the pirogues. Another Indian with a blazing torch followed him. It was getting dark fast now, and among the black shapes of the boats every little while lifted the black snout of an alligator. You could hear the alligators' jaws snapping shut. Far off their unseen brothers bellowed their dusk song with that noise of a hungry wind. The two Indians crouched in the bow of their pirogue. The one with the harpoon poised and flung it, his bracelets ringing. Jacques watched the uplifted arm black against the pale water and guessed he was after an alligator.

But when the harpoon had whistled through the air, the Indian leaned over and drew it lightly this way and that in the water. Jacques walked out to the edge of the bank to see better. It was a fish the man had caught. He was drowning it. Three times in all the harpoon sang through the air. It never missed. The two fishermen came bounding back on shore dangling three silversided fish. They made a fire right away and cooked the fish and brought them on a palmetto leaf to Jacques.

The smell of the hot fish only made Jacques feel more ill, but he was afraid to refuse it. It was dark now. He moved out of the circle of firelight carrying the palmetto platter gingerly and hid it under some leaves and twigs.

The Indians talked, never interrupting, never hurrying, sonorous and slow like alligator bulls. They spread a skin on the ground and made signs for Jacques to lie on it. Then one of them sat down beside him, put a hand on Jacques' shoulder and rocked him back and forth, back and forth. Why is he doing that, Jacques wondered. The movement made him restless and uneasy.

A whippoorwill was sounding his sad call in the black magnolia branches. Mosquitoes clustered in swarms thick about Jacques' face and hands, stabbing, stabbing till his skin felt as if it were on fire. At some time in the burning, uncomfortable dark the strange voices and that mysterious rocking motion stopped. Hot as he was, Jacques drew the thick-furred bearskin around his face to keep the mosquitoes off and fell into a troubled sleep.

When he waked next morning everything was still. All of the Indians except two were gone, and those two, one at each side of him, sat as silent as carved images in church. The canoes on the river, like the Indians, had vanished, and—yes—Jacques' gun was gone. He looked at the tree against which he had set his gun last night, and a little shudder ran down his spine. A savage will do anything for a gun, the Canadians had said.

The edge of a gourd cup pressed at his mouth. He set his teeth and motioned the Indian to take it away. He felt less than ever like swallowing that cold raw mush. They made signs to him to get up. He obeyed. One of them rolled up Jacques' bearskin and, shouldering it, set off at a trot. The other gave Jacques a little shove and they followed. They went inland, deeper and deeper into the woods. Jacques did the best he could to keep up, but his head ached and his knees were like water. Toward noon he stumbled and fell on a little slope all woven over with soft brown pine needles.

The only time in his life he had ever felt like this was in France a year ago last All Saints' Day. He had been very ill after that. The doctor had had to be called with his lancets and cupping instruments. The good priest had brought his own reliquary to hang about Jacques' neck while he said a novena for Jacques to get well. Every day the neighbors had come tapping at the kitchen door to ask in anxious whispers if Jacques was any better. The skipper had been away at sea at the time, but Aunt Gabrielle, her eyes red with sleeplessness and tears, had never left Jacques' side day or night.

Who would take care of him now, he wondered, if he should be ill.

The two Indians hardly looked at him. They set themselves imperturbably to felling a pine sapling by means of a girdling fire and a stone hatchet. It seemed hours before they got the tree down and the branches lopped, but they never hurried at all. Jacques kept dropping off to sleep. He waked after a while swaying gently this way and that.   The motion was far from unpleasant.   It was like being in a ship's hammock.   The wind made a sound like the sea.   He could almost believe he was in the *Palm Tree* going back home.   But he knew of course that the hammock was really a bearskin hung on a pine pole between copper-colored shoulders.

The wind came through the pine-trees spiced with resinous smells, and Jacques heard soft-shod running feet crunching gravel.   Day slipped into night and then into day again.   Jacques lost all track of time.   Sometimes the whispering feet went splashing through water. Sometimes on the edge of a river the bearskin hammock with Jacques inside was laid down on the ground while the Indian bearers spent hours making a raft of bundled canes.   Then the hammock and Jacques were lifted onto the raft, and the Indians swam across the river pushing the raft before them.   Dark-skinned shoulders glistening and wet look a little like porpoises wheeling along through water.

Now and then a gourd cup pressed at Jacques' mouth. He hated the raw reddish mush in the cup.   He thought thirstily of a drink of gooseberry jelly and water which Aunt Gabrielle had made to cool his fever.

After indefinite days through the unpeopled forest they came to an Indian village.   Seen in the twilight it seemed, to Jacques' fevered vision, hardly real.   The thatched huts spread dark and mysterious under the trees.   Fronting an open square rose a round temple with the shapes of strange beasts and birds on the roof and beside the portals: a great cock carved out of wood and stained as red as blood, and dragon-things and serpent-things and one puffed-out spotted toad-thing bigger than Jacques. One of the sculptured animals had a head like a sucking-pig's and a tail like a rat's and a pouch on its breast to carry its young in. On painted poles about the temple hung the scalps of the tribe's slain enemies. The hair on the scalps hung down like the mosses on Gulf Coast trees and, like the mosses, blew gently back and forth in the wind.

The people in the village didn't seem quite like men and women. They were all nearly naked. The women wore only bits of deerskin tied on like little petticoats with girdles woven of bright feathers and of animals' hair dyed different colors, and some wore leg-bands like garters with rattles strung on them. The men had queues or crests of red and yellow and black feathers plaited into the top-knots of hair left on their close-shaven polls, and they wore painted leather girdles from which dangled animals' tails and leather thongs loaded with all sorts of rattling, tinkling baubles. Except for that, the people all went as naked as your palm, their bare, dark thighs crashing through the leafy underbrush as easily as deer's legs. And they were all tattooed—the women as well as the men. The fantastic designs in bright colors pricked upon their breasts and limbs gave them a distorted appearance and made them, even when they smiled, grotesque and fearsome like their idols—the blood-red cock and the toad that was so many times bigger than life.

After dark all the people gathered in the open square. They planted poles in the ground, each with a bundle of reeds bound at the top as thick as a child's body, and

set fire to the reeds.   And then they danced in the leaping torch-light.

Jacques leaned his aching head against a tree-trunk
and watched them going round and round, in circles one
within the other, to a clamor of strange sounds:
the chanting of weird syllables, the beating of drums, the
clickety-click of chichicois, the jingle of bells and the
queer lot of odds and ends strung on the thongs dangling down the dancers' legs.   One young buck wore
three French skillets swinging like bell-clappers to clash
and ring each time he leaped in air.   One man played
on a wailing flute made of some animal's leg bone.   And
the leader of the dance had a whistle.   The drums were
made of skin stretched over clay pots half filled with
water.   The drums pounded all together and so steadily
that they sounded like a giant's heart beating.   The
medley of sounds and the stamping of feet seemed to
shake the hard-packed earth and make the leaves overhead quiver and sway.

The night was half gone when Jacques by signs got
his bearers to take him up from the ground and carry
him to a couch of woven cane inside one of the huts.
But even then he couldn't go to sleep, because his head
ached so and he couldn't shut the wild clashing echoes
out of his ears.

Next morning the bearers took up Jacques' litter and
pushed on their way, but at dusk they stopped in another
village.   And the next day, too.   To Jacques, the villages were all just alike, all dim and mysterious and all
with great torch-lit squares where howls and the stamping of feet sounded with drums and chichicois all night

long so you couldn't sleep. They stopped at villages only at night. Every time it was light again they moved on. After a while there were no more villages, only thick woods again day after day and deep green cane-brakes. Once in the night there was a great storm with thunder and lightning that made a dead pine, as tall and straight as a ship's mast, flame up to heaven like a mighty torch. The rain was cold and it felt good on Jacques' hot face. But afterwards his throat and chest hurt terribly.

At last he wasn't moving any more. He was again lying on a couch in an Indian hut. He felt the ridges of a woven cane mat against his bare flesh. It was night. There was a fire in the middle of the hut, and a horned man was dancing around it howling and shaking a chichicois. Over the fire was a bubbling pot from which came off a strange-smelling steam. Past the door on the beaten ground outside the hut hundreds of naked figures wove in and out to a wild rhythm. Jacques' head throbbed painfully with the pounding of drums and the thudding of feet. Feather crests passing across the flare of unseen torches printed shifting silhouettes, black on red.

The dancers stopped at last and sat down cross-legged in a circle on the ground. Inside the hut, the horned man dipped a conch shell into the pot and handed it to a youth with an owl's head over his brow. The youth went backward through the door, stooping low as if in reverence or fear. He carried the conch shell in both hands chanting something as he went, and stopped before someone who sat facing the door of the hut—the chief, perhaps, since his head-dress was inches higher than anyone else's. All the voices took up that wild chant then, and the man in the towering coronal took the conch shell, gulped a mouthful, held it while the chant lasted and spat it out on the ground. Then he gulped another great drink, which he swallowed.

The horned man left off stirring the pot, came toward the couch where Jacques was lying, and began to dance around it. The two horns fastened on the leather band about his brow curled back and downward. All his beard had been plucked out except two bristles under his nostrils and two just below on his chin. They were painted in four different colors. The face was painted, too, with black and red and yellow stripes across the nose onto the cheeks. The stripes wavered and ran together in fearful grimaces. A hand rose high in air and hung there. The hand held a cane knife.

The horned man danced nearer and nearer to the couch, howling and grimacing as he came. At last the hand with the knife in it hung just over Jacques' head. And then it swept down with a singing sound.

CHAPTER XIII

"Alali–o"

THE air felt soft and warm when Jacques waked up. It was like a coverlet woven of feathers. The shape of a low, narrow doorway was printed on an earthen floor by sunlight. Across the top of the open door a syca-more bough slanted downward. It hung there without rustling the least bit, and the leaves with the sun through them looked like thin stretched silk. They looked cool and pretty like a lady's parasol tilted up into the hot sun. Where had Jacques seen a parasol that color with the sun shining through it? It tired him to try to think. So he turned his face away from the door.

A gun stood leaning at the opposite wall. Beside it lay a bundle tied up in a pink-sprigged kerchief. The sight of the gun and the bundle was very comforting. Jacques didn't bother to discover why. He merely looked at his possessions and felt a healing in their near-ness. Over his body was spread a coverlet woven en-tirely of the iridescent head feathers of wild ducks. Hundreds and hundreds of ducks it must have taken to make that shimmering green coverlet. He stroked the long silky shag with his fingertips.

There was a sound of singing like a mocking-bird's, but not a mocking-bird's all the same. There was a

99

sweet smell, too—like a French garden in summer time.
After a little, Jacques got up. His legs were wobbly
but he could walk. He brought his bundle over to his
couch and opened it. It was just as it had been tied up.
None but a French woman could fold shirts like that,
roll stockings so neatly. Nobody had touched his
things since Marie had packed them. A bit of something metallic flashed out of the folded garments
and rolled down on the earth floor. It was a saint's
medal such as every peddler in France carried in his pack
to sell to devout peasants. Jacques picked it up and
held it on his palm. He sat on the edge of his couch
a long time looking at the little St. Christopher with
the boy on his shoulder high and safe above the silver
waves. He still heard that singing, sweet voice. He
dressed himself and went outside.

On each side of the door lay cane mats covered with
ripe plums drying in the sun. Across an open square
an old man reclined before his door working with a
little tool at a chunk of redstone cupped in his palm.
Closer to Jacques a woman sat under a sycamore tree.
A brown baby upright in a queer little envelope made
of reeds and skin swung from the branches over her
head. A vine rope tied to the swinging cradle hung
down in reach of the woman's hand. She gave it a
tug and, still singing, turned back to her work. She
was weaving a basket of split shining canes dyed different colors. The pattern she was weaving seemed familiar somehow. The woman spoke to Jacques as he
came out. He wanted to answer, and, surprisingly, the
word rose ready to his tongue:

"Alali-o."

He didn't know what the word meant, to be sure, or when precisely he had learned it. He knew only that it was a good word, a word to use in friendly greeting as a white man says good-morning or how-do-you-do. The Indian woman did not smile or show any surprise when Jacques answered her in her own tongue. She rose and went into the hut and brought out the cane mat from his couch and spread it down for him to lie on. Jacques smiled his gratitude and lay down on the mat. He saw now that his mat had a pattern of black angles and red lines threaded through yellow. It was the same design as that taking shape on the basket the woman was weaving. He turned to point out the similarity to her, but she was going away again.

Jacques reached for the vine rope of the baby's cradle and lay pulling it gently back and forth. The chunk of redstone at which the old man across the square was working was about the size of the Indian pipe-bowls Jacques had seen. That, no doubt, was what the old man was going to make.

When the woman came back, she set down on the ground beside Jacques a small earthen pot full of steaming sagamité with a horn spoon leaning in it. The sagamité had some of those fragrant fresh plums cooked all through it. Jacques had never tasted anything in all his life so good—no, not even cabbage soup in a French kitchen. He ate the last morsel, exploring the sides of the little pot carefully with the horn spoon.

He went to sleep after he had eaten. When he waked up next time the feather blanket lay over him again, light as a shining cloud.   The slanting sun stroked its iridescence to a gem-like fire.   The shadow of the syca-more stretched far beyond the hut now.   Yellow jack-ets hung greedily over the red plums on the mats.   The old man had disappeared from before his door.   The woman and the baby were nowhere to be seen.   Jacques yawned and stretched and stood up.   He didn't feel quite so wobbly.   He fanned the yellow jackets away, caught up a handful of plums and ate them.   He heard voices and wandered in the direction they came from. He crossed the wide beaten square, passed by a temple-like house with painted wooden images of birds and animals up over it, threaded his way among smaller huts, round like bee-hives or like French windmills, straggling off through the trees, and came to the edge of a young cornfield.

Boys were running about through the field, and on a scaffolding at one side were some old women and the same old man Jacques had seen earlier in the day.   The old man, who wore a woven white robe and still busied his hands with his carving, was talking in a loud flow-ing voice.   The corn was waist high.   The wind made little waves go running across it.   A crow dropped down from a high pine and sailed low over the field of rippling green.   One of the old women began to screech and throw her thin arms about.   She pointed at the crow's black shadow slipping across the young green corn and screamed and screamed.

Two boys reached for arrows from the quivers slung at their backs.   One of them used an ordinary arrow and bow.   But the other fitted an arrow of a very dif-

ferent kind into a cane cylinder more than five feet long
and, pointing the shaft at the flying crow, puffed out his
cheeks and blew into the cane as hard as he could.   The
boy with the bow and the boy with the blowgun took aim
at exactly the same moment.   And the two arrows flew
away together.   The crow stopped, rolled over and
over, and plunged under the sea of corn.

From all over the field boys went running, to see, of
course, which arrow it was that had brought the crow
down.   It would be easy to tell because the blowgun
arrow was tufted with down nearly half its length.
Jacques wasn't strong enough to go running like the
rest.   But he was very much excited.   He stood still,
his heart thumping against his shirt.   He wanted the
blowgun boy to win.   And he wanted it with an in-
tensity that surprised him.

The boys came back across the field.   The boy with
the bow lagged far behind.   The boy with the blowgun
marched ahead with the dead crow in his hand.   An
admirer was carrying his blowgun for him.   Jacques
felt a lump come in his throat as they drew near him.
He wanted to speak to the boy, to congratulate him.
But how could he?   Another minute and the boy would
have passed altogether.

Jacques wet his lips.

"Oh," he cried, just "Oh."

The Indian boys all turned and looked at him.   They
didn't laugh as white-skinned boys would have done.
They looked at him gravely, politely.   They didn't
seem surprised at his calling out to them.   The blowgun boy spoke the greeting word which Jacques didn't

really understand but to which, curiously, he knew the proper answer:

"Alali-o," Jacques said quickly, smiling.

The Indian boy was taller than Jacques by at least an inch, as tall in fact as his own slender blowgun and as straight. Besides his belted quiver slung at his shoulder, he wore nothing at all but a blue jay's wing plaited into his shining black hair, and about his waist a red leather girdle with pendant gewgaws swinging and tinkling from it like the crystal fringe of a French chandelier. His eyes were as black as buttons, but they weren't hard looking like buttons. They were soft and liquid instead. His gaze rested in Jacques' for a long moment.

Then he pulled the head of the crow through his belt, and, turning, took his blowgun from his follower's hands and held it toward Jacques. He offered it upright like a spear, one end resting on the ground, and at the same moment slipped the strap of his quiver over his head and extended it in his other hand, full as it was of curious tufted arrows each cunningly and patiently made. There was no mistaking his meaning. The blowgun was a gift.

Jacques flushed and laughed shyly as his fingers closed on the smooth cane shaft of the blowgun and on the leather strap of the quiver.

Jacques felt a curious thrill along his spine. He had never had a friend his own age in all his life. He hurriedly wriggled his head through the quiver strap to get his hand free and fished out of his pocket the silver St. Christopher. Maybe it was a queer present to give an Indian boy who certainly couldn't know anything at all about the good saint and what a protection against harm his image was. But it was all Jacques had to give.

And the Indian boy liked it. He held it on his palm and stroked it with his fingers. And all the other boys bent over his hand and stroked it with their fingers as though they envied him. Then the new owner of the little silver saint caught up one of the leather strings to his girdle and tied the medal to it hard between two fawns' trotters and a dried turkey spur.

Another floating shadow laid its menace on the corn just then, and the old women on the platform set up their screams of alarm The boys sped off, stretching their bows as they went. Jacques, left alone, stood smiling to himself.

Just in front of him out of the thick cornstalks lifted a pair of great curving horns framing a face striped laterally in red and yellow and black with bristles in four colors about the mouth. Jacques was too weak to run even if he hadn't been encumbered as he was. He clutched the tall blowgun against him to steady his shaking legs. The horned man bent so near that Jacques could feel his breath along his cheeks. The man put out his fingers and touched Jacques' temples.

All day Jacques had forgotten those scars on his temples made last night by the cane knife. Even now he couldn't bear to remember them. He shut his eyes and waited, sick and faint. But nothing happened and he opened his eyes again. The horned man was rubbing his own forehead now, and the lips between the painted bristles emitted a little gentle purring sound.   Jacques didn't know in the least what that meant.   How could he?   But it seemed like an apology, somehow, or perhaps an explanation.   Jacques managed to smile and nod up into the striped face.   And it withdrew, grinning.

The sun was going down now beyond the rustling corn.   The boys had shot another crow.   The air was filled with treble shouts of triumph.   Through the trees beyond the huddled houses, the fires were already lighted and the drums were calling to dance. Over the prairie in other villages dim as phantoms other fires flared and other drums pounded faint and far as an echo or as a great heart beating under the round breasts of the prairie.

Jacques turning "homeward" had a strange sense of newness like a baby just born.   It was as if everything that had ever happened before to-day was of no more account to him.   His life in France and even at the fort on the river was too far off and much too different to matter here.   All he knew that he could use now was one word he had picked up somehow unconsciously as he must have learned the pattern on his mat while he had been ill.   He laughed and spoke his one word aloud as he walked along—"Alali-o, Alali-o" over and over to the beat of the calling drums.

CHAPTER XIV

THE LITTLE CHIEF

THE horned man stood on the roof of the town house waving his arms and shouting up into the sky. He was ordering the clouds to pass on because corn needs dry weather to grow in. If the fields had been thirsty he would have boiled a certain sacred herb called the "most beloved plant" and summoned all the people to sing and dance around the bubbling pot. And that would have been a signal for the rolling clouds to stop and let the rain down.

Jacques sat on his mat in the shade of the sycamores, eating with a horn spoon from a wooden platter balanced on his crossed legs. Between mouthfuls he watched the antics of the figure against the hot blue sky. Beyond the doorway of the chief's house a sick girl lay on her couch. Her eyes were open. She, too, seemed to be watching the horned man. Somewhere out of sight a woman was pounding nuts and over beyond the town house sounded the shouts of the young men and the thud of the stone wheel they were always rolling from morning till night. In the square a crowd of little boys were shooting arrows at a fistful of hay tied at the top of a red-painted pole. Before his door as usual sat the old man—the mythkeeper they called him

—who was still carving at his pipe, if it really was a pipe he intended to make. Whatever it was it never seemed any nearer completion. Jacques had a queer feeling that the old man—the mythkeeper—always had been there before his door and always would be, and that the shapeless hunk of stone cradled in his palm never would look any different, although he chipped at it so patiently with his little flint-tipped tool day after day.

How slowly time passed. Two or three years Monsieur de Bienville had said Jacques must live with the Indians. As though two years and three were very much the same thing! But even a summer seems endless when no bells or guns mark off the hours and the days are all just alike. There weren't even any meal-times. When anybody got hungry he just told one of the women and she served up whatever it was she happened to be cooking in her pot: sweet potatoes Jacques had to-day and very good they were, too, dressed with milk of pounded hickory nuts.

The summer *was* passing of course. One way to tell was by remembering back to the time when wild plums were ripe and Jacques had known only one Indian word. The corn had been only waist high then. Now it towered above the great chief's coronal of eagle feathers. The stalks were as thick as a man's arm. The old women who went into the fields every day to pinch the young ears and feel the drying silk between thumb and palm licked their lips with satisfaction at the way the corn had ripened. It was just about ready to eat now, but the old women wouldn't let anybody touch it.

THE HORNED MAN STOOD ON THE ROOF OF THE TOWN—HOUSE.

They believed it would be some sort of sin to eat one grain of the new corn before the next new moon.

Instead of one word Jacques knew lots now. In fact he was getting so he could understand much of what was said. He could talk pretty well, too, by piecing out with gestures the way the Indians themselves did when travelers from distant tribes and other tongues came among them. Jacques was learning the language rather quickly. If only he could get along as fast with the things the Indian boys thought worth while!

Every morning at sunrise one of the old men stood in the trodden square and called the young people up. They waked with as much noise as a treeful of birds and went streaming out of the village to a near-by water-filled clay hole for a swim. Sometimes they went all the way to the river instead. The women went along to teach the babies new-released from their cradle-boards. Jacques, feeling as helpless as the brown, splut-tering babies, had at last nerved himself to fling off his French shirt and breeches and wade in, but he could do little more than fight at the water with his arms and legs and choke and strangle. The Indian boys his age —and even the girls—slid through the water with no more noise than a fish or a pirogue; except, of course, at the river, where they cavorted and beat up fountains on purpose to keep the alligators off the babies while they were learning.

After weeks of practice, it seemed to Jacques he had made no progress in anything that required physical skill. He still couldn't manage blowgun or bow well enough to be allowed to police the cornfields with the other boys his age. He could have used his French gun of course, but the old men forbade that—unfairly, Jacques thought—and kept him back every day with the youngsters who were being taught to use the bow.

The horned man leaped down from the town-house and came springing across the square past the young archers. The sick girl sat up on her couch, staring. Jacques set his platter on the ground and dragged his mat a little farther off. He didn't want to see the horned man enter the sick girl's hut.

He knew how it would be: the twisted roots and seed-pods sprinkled in the pot boiling over the fire; the chichicois; the prancing; perhaps a live snake writhing and crooking in air before it settled around the girl's bare waist; perhaps a chant calling the fish spirits to come and cool the fever; the cane knife biting into her flesh at the temples; the lips between the painted tufts of beard coming down to suck at the bleeding wounds. And then, if she didn't get better, all the people would be summoned, as when Jacques had been ill, to feast and dance before her door to drive off the evil spirits of disease.

The horned man surely meant no cruelty—no more than the doctor at home in France who came with his painful lancets and cupping instruments when people were sick; no more than the priest who hung his own reliquary about your neck and said novenas to make the pain go away. But all the same Jacques moved out of range of that open door. Behind him, pebbles in a hollow gourd went clickety-click and the horned man began to wail the sacred alligator song.

Slipped in between the trying sounds came a familiar,

agreeable jingling. The Indian boys made no noise at
all with their bare feet. But you could usually hear them
coming by the sound of the gewgaws they wore strung
at their girdles. Fawns' trotters and dried turkey claws
make a hard rattling noise not unlike a chichicois, but
a little silver medal has a ringing tone all its own.
Jacques looked up smiling.

"You have come?" he exclaimed in the Indian language.

The boy who wore the gage of Jacques' admiration
among the other trophies at his belt was sweating and
panting from some recent trial of strength. He had
barely breath enough to answer:

"Alali-o—I am here."

Jacques pushed the half-emptied platter toward him.
He fingered the medley at his girdle, found a spoon of
buffalo horn, untied it, and without another word began
to eat. He hadn't any name—none of the Indian boys
had real names until they were old enough to win them
by heroism of some sort. He went by any one of a
half-dozen fanciful titles which his fellows gave him.
They called him the Apprentice Warrior or Junior
Chief or Little Chief, because in whatever was going on
among them he was always the leader.

He could swim best, wrestle best, run farthest.
When the boys stirred up wasps' nests with long switches
he could stand still enduring the stings upon his naked
breast and thighs longer than anybody else. When
they all came back at night from policing the cornfields
he was sure to bear the heaviest load of squirrels and
crows and blackbirds strung about his waist. If the
young men ever admitted any boy to that difficult game

they were always playing beyond the town house, it was certain to be the Little Chief because he could roll the heavy stone wheel almost as far and hurl the staff almost as straight as they themselves.

The Little Chief stopped after two spoonfuls and pushed the platter inquiringly toward Jacques. Jacques shook his head and laughed. He was sure the Little Chief after his latest feat, whatever it had been, must be hungrier than he, who had been doing nothing more fatiguing than archery practice with the eight-year-olds.

Jacques hoped that when the Little Chief got through eating he might stay and talk a little. The Little Chief must know a lot of interesting things. He was one of the chosen few to whom the mythkeeper, with the help of those strange notched sticks and shell bead chaplets which served him as books serve a French priest, was teaching the traditions of the tribe.

But the Little Chief was a person of few words. He had never once attempted conversation with Jacques, nor did he linger now after his hunger was satisfied. He scraped the platter, wiped his horn spoon on a handful of sycamore leaves, and sprang to his feet murmuring the brief formula of farewell:

"I go."

"You do," Jacques agreed as was customary and polite, but he couldn't help sighing a little.

He watched the Little Chief go springing across the square and disappear around the town house. Then he picked up his bow and quiver and took his way back into the square to join the little boys at their target practice again.

CHAPTER XV

THE GREEN-EARED MOON

THE month when the corn ripened was called the Green-eared Moon—as in France one would have said July or August. It was greeted with elaborate and mystic ritual. First, all the people cleaned their houses and burned every grain of the old corn and all of their old soiled deerskins and breechclouts. Then the square was sprinkled with sand and decked with green boughs and armfuls of blossoming trumpet vine and all the many-colored wild flowers that gemmed the prairies.

Jacques didn't see what happened then, because no one but the warriors could stay in the square while the new holy fire was being kindled. A boy who forgot and ran too near after the ceremony began was caught up on the instant and dry-scratched: his naked back set aflame by the horned man's gar's-tooth comb and the mercy of cool water denied him. The boy didn't cry out, but his lips drew back in a goblin grin of pain.

In the first days of the Green-eared Moon, everybody fasted. But at last came the day when the old women gathered the ripe corn and the young women ran about between the houses each shielding with her palm a smoking brand from the holy fire. And then the bright flames woke before every door and the good smells started and soon the feasting began.

Some of the new corn was roasted whole in the ear. Some was pounded with young green chestnuts and packed back into the green corn blades, where corn and chestnuts cooked together. Some of it was mixed with bears' oil and molded into thin cakes and baked on flat stones in the ashes. There was sagamité, of course, cooked in every sort of way, with fresh fruit and dry, with beans, with squash, with venison. There were peaches and apples heaped high in bright new baskets. There were rabbits and squirrels roasted whole and sweet potatoes moistened with hickory milk. There was watermelon with an inside like rose-colored snow, which melted in the mouth as if it actually were snow and left after it a cool, delicious taste, like—what was it like? Jacques was eating his third watermelon when he remembered Aunt Gabrielle's cooling drink of gooseberry jelly mixed with water.

The warriors went about new-painted with vermilion and ocher, their heads nodding with their finest feathers and horns. Hot as it was, some of them got out their most treasured deerskin mantles, dressed as soft as chamois and drawn all over with bright-colored pictures of their exploits in war and hunt. They wore bracelets of feathers or beads or deer-ribs bent and polished, and necklaces of bears' teeth or shell beads with engraved shell pendants. The women dancers fastened tortoise shells to their garter-like leg bands, filled with clattering gravel stones, and hundreds of small wild hoofs and all the bright and tinkling metal

things their chiefs had brought up from the French settlement. In some of the dances they wore masks made
of big gourds grotesquely carved and painted.

Dancing went on all night long and all day, too, until
the ground was trodden into furrows. People from
the neighboring villages came and without a word of
greeting fell to dancing. The chief's daughter got
up from her couch and began to dance with all her might
as if she had never been ill in her life. Sometimes the
dancers let the rattling things down their legs make
a deafening clatter. But sometimes they moved so that
they made no noise at all. They danced about great
bonfires, shielding their faces from the glare with fans
of turkey feathers. And now and then a kick from
a dancer sent flames and sparks leaping up into the high
tree branches.

When the dancers stopped to rest, they gathered
about the old mythkeeper in his woven white robe, firelight reddening his wise, wrinkled face. And he willingly laid aside his carving. And, fingering those chaplets on which a rattlesnake rattle stood for a war, perhaps, a point of buck horn for a great storm out of the
Gulf, he recited the oldest and most beloved traditions
of their people.

A singer came up from the country of their former
enemies—those with whom the Iron Hand and Messieurs d'Iberville and de Bienville had contrived to have
them smoke the calumet of peace—and sitting down
close beside their holy fire like a blood brother sang all
the songs of his people, their one-time enemies. Some
of the songs were so old that they were half-forgotten

now and some were so new that no alien ear had ever heard them before.

One afternoon there was a great ball-play out upon the prairie. People gathered from the sister villages of the nation. Many brought all their skins and ornaments to wager on the game. The players were naked and painted all over, one team with white clay, one with red. They carried in their hands long scoop-like rackets, called ball-sticks. And when they ran and leaped in the sunshine after the stuffed deerskin ball their tails of dyed and plaited silk grass blew out behind them.

One night the warriors sat in a circle about the red-painted pole while the chief went to strike it with his great, edged war-club, or "headbreaker," and chanted:

> The lightning clove an oak-tree
> And so was I born,
> Sinewy and hard as oak-wood,
> Swift-leaping as the sky-fire
> That springs from cloud to cloud
> On summer nights.
> The lightning was my father,
> An oak-tree was my mother . . .
> Who shall gainsay it?

He paused and looked about him. The warriors loosed a great *hou* of approval from their chests and shook their chichicois. The chief struck the pole again with his club.

> The thunder of my bow
> Scatters fear
> Like a storm from the Gulf.

My uncle, the wind,
Himself has winged my arrows.
My father has touched their tips
With his own fire
That they may carry the death spark
Straight to the hearts of my enemies . . .
Does any man doubt it?

When he sat down, the warriors rose in the order of their distinction and chanted each his own prowess. Even the boys were allowed to strike the pole and tell, not what they had done of course, but what they were going to do when they were men. If a boy was timid and spoke poorly the chiefs and warriors were silent and looked at the ground. But if one was fearless and eloquent they applauded him.

When the Little Chief's turn came, he stood as straight as the red pole itself, flung his chin high and with an odd shining look in his black eyes told of all he dreamed of doing for the glory of his people. When he finished, the warriors and chiefs fetched great whoops of approval out of their deep chests blazoned all over with the insignia of their brave deeds.

Jacques dug his nails against his palms and stole away by himself. He had a feeling that was part pride and part pain. He hated to think of the Little Chief wearing a warrior's swan-feather crown on his head and scalps at his belt.

He walked slowly away through the trees. Behind him in the square, the drums and chichicois and voices took up the rhythm of the Red Ant Dance. It was quite dark under the trees, but beyond them it was nearly

as bright as day.   The moon was a week old now.   The
ground in front of the house like a temple was spattered with brightness.   And the wooden bear with a
man's head up over the door was black against the
shining sky.   A mocking-bird lit on the bear-thing's
head and began to sing.

Jacques walked across the island of light and, still
thinking of the Little Chief's speech, curiously fingered
the dried scalps hanging on the poles before the temple-
like house.   A black shadow lay on the silver ground
when Jacques turned around, but it was instantly swallowed up in the tree-shadows.   Somebody had been
watching him.   Would the Indians call what Jacques
had just done some sort of desecration?   He remembered the boy he had seen dry-scratched the day the holy
fire was kindled.   He froze into stillness.   Fireflies
threaded the close-woven shade.   Far away beat the
drums, the chichicois, the stamping feet, the chanting
voices, endless and mysterious.   A wind bent branches
rustling downward over Jacques' head.   The dried
scalps rattled crisply against the poles.

Jacques' straining ears caught a vagrant hint of
sound, a mere flash, swift as a firefly and glinting like
a firefly, too—such a sound precisely as a saint's medal
makes swinging like a little bell-clapper.   Jacques
laughed aloud with relief when he heard the sound by
which he always recognized the Little Chief's nearness.
He flung himself into the dark toward the faint glint
of sound.   His arms closed on a naked body.   The
Little Chief taken unaware tumbled backward, but his
arms closed around Jacques and Jacques, too, went

down. The two boys rolled over and over like pup-
pies. But only for a moment. The Little Chief hurried to drag Jacques out into the moonlight where he
could piece out speech with gestures, as needful to make
Jacques understand.

Listen. In Jacques' own tribe far away across the
ocean had they a mythkeeper?

Jacques hesitated.

"Why, yes," he said after a moment. "A priest we
call him."

"And has he taught you the old beloved legends of
your people?"

"Yes," said Jacques still puzzled.

"I will teach you all I know," said the Little Chief
panting with eagerness, "if you will tell me stories of
the white men's country."

Jacques laughed aloud and flung his arm around the
Little Chief's shoulder. Oh, he had enough tales to
last for months: all the priest's stories from the lives of
saints and heroes; all Aunt Gabrielle's chimney-corner
tales of Hop o' My Thumb and his company; all
Jacques' own adventures with the skipper in the *Swallow*. He could tell of the château they visited the time
they took the anchovies from the north coast of Brittany up the River Loire; of the walled town where
Jacques' home was and the king's high-towered arsenal;
of ships and sailors and Mardi Gras, which is the French
people's Green-eared Moon, when they put on masks
and sing and dance in the streets.

CHAPTER XVI

Persimmon Bread

Jacques thought it must be toward the end of September when they began burning the country over. The crisp air came spiced with the charred fragments of leaves and grass. A mighty sound of popping came out of the canebrakes as though whole armies of musketeers lay in ambush here. All the woods grew dark with smoke. And through the tall grass and golden-rod over the prairies waved little red flags of flame. A small rain came to wet the singed prairies and new grass sprang up soft as down to tempt the deer. The ground was suddenly spangled over with mushrooms as thick as stars in the Milky Way—the White Dog's

Road, the Indians called it. Grapes ripened, purple and amber. Sweet-gum oozed fragrant resin and its leaves turned the color of rich port wine. Hickory-nut-trees turned clear yellow instead, and that gave, in the places where they stood, an odd effect of sunlight in the smoky forests. Light seemed to come, too, from the persimmons strung like gold lanterns along bare branches. The mocking-birds burst into a second season of song.

There was no more work to be done in the fields now. The corn and the dried fruit and the barbecued scimitar-like slices of pumpkin were all stored in the cribs set like French dove-cotes on high stilts, well polished to discourage mice. The men hunted a little but mostly they busied themselves getting ready for the great winter hunt. All day long they polished arrows or labored at deer-head decoys stretched over hooped laths, the antlers patiently hollowed out so they should weigh upon the hunting-pack scarcely more than a dry hollow gourd. The women again swung their corn-carriers against their shoulders by the deerskin forehead straps and scattered over the country to reap a second harvest. The boys, Jacques and the Little Chief in their midst, went along to help fill the hampers. They swept up the starry mushrooms out of the meadows, gleaned wild rice in the marshes, disputed the right of the bears to the juicy muscadines festooning the high trees, and went into the groves where all the ground was fat with hickory nuts and the bright persimmons hung in air as big as hen's eggs and as mellow as good French butter.

The women squeezed the persimmons over cane sieves to get the skin and seeds out, rolled the paste into broad flat cakes and roasted them over fires in the woods. They hung up the big blue muscadines and dried them on the stem like sweet raisins from Greece.

Soon flocks of wild pigeons came flying so thick that they clouded over the copper sun. Swans and ducks and geese gathered about the marshes and lakes. Every low place was like a fair in the market square of a busy French town. Stray hunters unwise enough to camp near any water could not sleep for the noise the wild fowl made. The ducks and geese have chiefs, the Indians said, and "old wise men" who meet every fall in their council house in the far north to decide when the tribe shall move south, just as the Indians themselves had leaders who fixed the time for setting out northward on the winter hunt.

There never had been a time when fowl had been so plentiful—at least the notched sticks and shell-bead chaplets of the mythkeeper carried the record of none. The boys with torches of blazing lightwood knots went through the woods at night and knocked down the roost-ing pigeons out of the trees by the bagful. In the daytime they took turkey skins dressed with the heads on and lay down behind fallen trees until the turkeys stepped mincingly out of the deeper woods in search of ripe nettle seed or red acorns. Then they lifted the decoys up on their fists and gobbled like turkeys to entice their game near enough to be caught.

The Little Chief stuffed a duck skin with straw and set it afloat on a pond, and when the ducks that were

flying over settled around it he swam under water, as
noiselessly as an eel, seized the ducks' feet, tucked the
heads under his belt, and swam ashore with them alive
and squawking.

The women wanted all the down feathers they could
get for making blankets and shawls. They wove the
feathers, as the wigmakers of France wove hair, on
nets of coarse bark thread till the nets were covered
all over on both sides with silky bright shag. The
women couldn't have too many duck feathers and the
boys themselves were very fond of roast duck. Jacques,
lips twisting on a little rueful smile, wished he could
have shared some of his with good Monsieur Bosset.
Did Monsieur Bosset, he wondered wistfully, still boast
as much as ever of the way they cook duckling at Rouen?

Jacques and the Little Chief were really friends now.
They were never separated. When the sun came burning up beyond the blue bare treetops, they went running
together over the frosty ground to swim in the ice-cold
river. And at night when the warm, crowded town
house was noisy with chichicois and dancing feet and
dim with smoke of pipes and lightwood knots, they lay
on one bearskin and whispered together. The Little
Chief never got tired of hearing Jacques talk about the
white men's country and, good as his word, he gave in
exchange one after another of the mythkeeper's stories
exactly as he had learned them.

Now it was a tale of the Ancient of Terrapins " . . .
not the little helpless terrapin we have in these days but
the first of all terrapins, mighty and heavy as a bear."
Now it was a story about a Sint-holo, the sacred horned

snake which lived along big creeks or in caves: "Once, the old men say, a hunter came upon a Sint-holo fighting with the Thunder . . . " Or it was the story of the Nameless Young Man: "There was once a young man who had no name, they say. Unluckily for him the tribe had smoked the calumet of peace with all its enemies. So the young man could not go out to war and get a man's name for people to call him by or a swan-feather crown for his temples. This was a matter of grief and shame to his parents and to the maiden who loved him and to the young man, too. For, though he grew to be as tall and strong as the great chief himself, still he had to go on lighting the warriors' pipes for them like a boy and heaping the lightwood knots in the square for the fires at evening . . . "

Story after story they told each other, and they had other things to talk about, besides. More than anything else now they talked about the winter hunt. They were both going, everybody was in fact—except a half-dozen ancients no longer fit to travel—even the myth-keeper, old as he was, and the babies who would have to ride like corn in baskets against the women's shoulders. Jacques was to carry his gun. No other boy had a gun of course—not even half of the warriors had any. Jacques was thankful now for the edict which had seemed so hard last summer. But for the old men he'd have wasted all of his powder and shot in the corn-fields and he would have had none left now. As it was, his powder horn was barely half full and his shot pouch all too flabby. In the brief hour he had tarried at the French fort before setting off again with the Indians,

nobody had thought to replenish his ammunition. So
precious was ammunition hereabout that the braves
made shot molds of clay and melted up everything metal
they had got from the French: skillets and kettles, even
nails and buttons.

Jacques had just twenty rounds left. He and the
Little Chief counted the shot a hundred times, turning
the bag up carefully over a gourd cup and fingering the
balls of lead as greedily as if they had been minted
doubloons. It was well understood that the Little
Chief was to fire ten shots and Jacques ten. They
couldn't spare one shot for practice, but the Little
Chief over and over went through the motions of loading and firing. They were in sworn agreement to use
arrows whenever possible. And they would disregard
the meaner sort of game altogether—a bear or so, perhaps, but no rabbits or squirrels and no beaver.

"Anybody can kill a beaver," the Little Chief said
scornfully. And from the talk in the town-house at
night it was clear that all the men were of his opinion.

One of the women took her needle of heron's bone
and her deer-sinew thread and fashioned a pair of moccasins for Jacques. The mythkeeper put down his still
unfinished pipe-bowl to make for him a "deer-call" out
of a bit of cane. And he taught Jacques as many of the
seven ancient songs to call up deer as were now remembered:

> Deer, deer, come sweeten your tongue
> On the fat juicy acorns
> Lying here around me. . . .

And:

> Nearer and nearer I creep in my deer mask—
> Where are you hiding, deer?
> Are you drinking there by the stream
> Out of sight among the tall ferns?
> Or are you lying in yonder shady grove?
> If that is where you are,
> I shall find you, deer.
> I shall steal upon you
> In my well-made deer mask.
> I shall cry:
> Awake, arise, stand up—
> The hunter is here with his arrows.

Even the horned man searched in his pouch among the seed pods of swamp flag and the bits of twisted roots for a charm to give Jacques. He drew out first a root of the plant called deer-tail, but he put it back and looked further. He found at last a wisp of velvet from the horns of a young deer, over which he mumbled a charm—the very best talisman, the Little Chief declared, not only for deer but for any sort of game.

Jacques grinned at the Little Chief's solemn faith. But he tucked the downy scrap into his shot pouch all the same.

At last the chiefs and old wise men met in the town house and decided it was time to go. The hunters fasted every day for three days and each night when they dreamed of any animal they believed it was the game they were sure to kill. The women made ready the usual traveling equipment: the deerskins to sleep on, the warm buffalo coverings, the little bags of reddish parched meal and a gourd cup apiece to stir up the cold gruel in.

The sun was just coming up when they stepped out from the shelter of the trees and houses. The sky was red and purple across the round-humped prairie. The ground was covered all over with frost that crumpled like starched lace under Jacques' new moccasins. Carrying his gun on his shoulder and munching the barbecued persimmon loaf which he and the Little Chief had just broken in half between them, he felt tingling and ecstatic. He had felt like that once before—when was it? Oh, yes, to be sure, it was the day Monsieur d'Iberville had said he might come along as ship's boy to the New World and dowered him with a great bundle of fine clothes from the king. What a child he had been!

CHAPTER XVII

The White Deer

THE place where they pitched their winter camp was eight sleeps as the Indians reckoned, or eight days' journey, away from home, in a grove of chestnuts on the southern slope of a very high hill, with a clear spring flowing in a ravine below it. As soon as they arrived the men set to building shelters of bark and evergreen boughs. The women opened the travel-packs. Jacques and the Little Chief were sent with a skin bag to fetch water from the spring. They came upon bear tracks. Jacques, by some incredible chance, was the first to see them. He guessed they were the footprints of a man walking barefoot, but the Little Chief stooping found the print of claws at the ends of the toes. Jacques dropped the water-bag to fly for his gun.

"Wait," said the Little Chief. How did they know it was not an ambush? These were rich hunting grounds. Their northern enemies sometimes came here.

"But you said yourself it was bears' claws," argued Jacques, almost dancing with impatience.

Bears' claws can be fastened on men's feet. Just last winter in these very hunting grounds an unwary hunter had been enticed to his death that way. The

Little Chief cautiously followed the tracks to the foot
of a tall elm which had a great hollow about forty feet
up and the bark deeply scratched as by claws climbing
up and down. The Little Chief laid his ear close to
the tree and Jacques did, too. They heard a low
hum-hum-hum. At last the Little Chief nodded—yes,
it was a bear. Jacques threw down the water-sack and
ran back up the slope.

At the camp he ran straight to the tree where his
gun leaned, calling out the tidings as he ran. They
all gathered about him to hear the particulars. And
one of the old men promptly ordered Jacques not to
touch his gun. With every man in camp and every
quiver full of arrows that was perhaps mere common
sense. But Jacques was terribly disappointed

However, there was no time to mope. He had to
guide them to the bear tree, and as soon as they got there
he and the other boys had to gather some dried rotten
wood which holds fire well and tie it into bundles with
strips of bark. The men half-felled a near-by sapling
and made it lean like a ladder over against the bear tree.
Then one of the young men fastened the bundles of
dried wood about his girdle, took a long stick in his
hand, and climbed up the leaning sapling. He set fire
to the bundles of wood one by one and with his stick
poked them down into the hollow. Almost at once
they could hear the bear snuffing in the tree. The
women and boys were made to stand back and the men
got ready with stretched bows in case the man who had
been chosen to shoot first should merely wound the
bear and he should turn upon them—a wounded bear

is very dangerous.   At last the fire got too hot inside
the tree and the bear came out.   He climbed down
backward like a man.   A bow twanged and he toppled,
a single arrow swaying like a rooted reed just behind
his shoulder.   He was as big as a French carriage horse,
and as soft and black as if a velvet pall had been flung
over him.

Some of the women ran up to the dead bear with their
keen-edged cane knives, and the rest hurried back to
the camp to stir up the fires and get the kettles on.
The hunters went off to try their luck at getting a deerskin to hold the bear fat.   Soon the camp in the chestnut grove was perfumed with the smell of roasting and
boiling bear meat.   It smelled good, too, after eight
days of cold meal-and-water gruel.   And it was aston-
ishing how good it did taste at last eaten without salt
or bread or even sagamité.

They were hardly done eating when one of the hunters came strolling into camp.

"Have you then killed a deer so quickly?" his wife
cried out.

He merely nodded his head back over his shoulder to
show her in what direction it lay, so she could go and
get it.

But the other hunter was not so lucky.   He did not
get back all that night.   Next day the old men had
Jacques and the Little Chief keep up a fire at the edge of
the chestnut grove as a signal.   All day the two boys
talked about the lost hunter and wondered what had
become of him.   Jacques told the Little Chief about
Monsieur Bosset and how he had been lost so long that

he had almost starved to death and had dug his own grave. The Little Chief told him all the details of the hunter who last winter had been enticed to his death by supposed bear tracks. And the Little Chief told, too, how sometimes the Little People, who lived in the woods, carried you off and kept you and taught you all sorts of things. Some people they taught how to get deer and those men always became great hunters afterwards. Some they taught the secrets of roots and seed-pods and these, when they returned to their own people, were able like the horned man to cure disease and even to make rain come. When it was a child who was carried off, the parents never went to look for him, because they knew the Little People would take care of him and when he was brought back he would be a lot wiser than when he went away.

Late that afternoon they saw the lost hunter come bounding across the ravine below. Eager to hear what could have kept him all this while, the two boys ran out to meet him. He brushed them aside like troublesome mosquitoes. He did not slacken his long swinging trot to hear their questions but bounded straight past them and their signal fire up into the woods where the camp was. Hard at his heels they saw him brush aside his wife, too, when she ran joyfully to meet him with a platter of smoking venison. He could hardly have failed to be hungry. He had been gone since yesterday morning. His empty meal pouch flapped at his thigh like a squeezed out rag. But he pushed that platter of odorous steaming meat out of his way as he had thrust off the two boys, and stepped in front of the mythkeeper sitting on a skin mat beside the fire.

"I have no hunger for meat," the hunter said, the ribs beneath his bare skin rounding out like hoops with his pumping breath. "My hunger is for understanding."

The mythkeeper murmured a mild greeting and signed for a skin to be spread for the hunter. Then he returned to his carving till the other should have got his breath. Everybody pressed in close about the two, because it was plain from the hunter's bearing that he had had some strange adventure.

"I have often hunted through this country," said the hunter at last in a low, surprised sort of voice. "I know it well. Yesterday I set off to go to a certain stream where the deer come to lick the salty moss that grows on the rocks. I had little more than left the camp, the sun was still high overhead . . ." here he made a gesture to show its exact angle. " . . . when I came to a place I had never seen before, an open valley between two hills like high walls. Just as I was turning about to retrace my steps and find the stream I was looking for, I saw on the ridge before me many deer together marching with an even pace like warriors. I saw them very plainly against the sky. At their head was a deer all white. He marched always in front. It was as if the others dared not go before him. . . ."

Here the hunter's voice broke, and although it was a very chill evening he caught up the empty meal pouch dangling at his belt and wiped sweat off his brow. His eyes left the mythkeeper's face and searched the other faces drawn close about in the twilight. Maybe he wanted to see if they believed him. Somewhere a man grunted, incredulously, Jacques thought.

"Is it true?" Jacques whispered to the Little Chief. "Are there some white deer who lead the others?"

But the mythkeeper motioned for silence. The hunter filled his great hooped chest with breath and went on:

"The herd walked along the crest of the hill and seemed to be making toward a defile between two overhanging rocks. I ran along the bottom of the valley as fast as I could, hoping to cut them off there and kill the white deer and bring his skin home to prove what I had seen. But as I ran up under the overhanging rocks the whole herd got away. It was strange where they could have gone to so quickly, for all the farther side of that hill was bare of trees. It was covered all over with sharp little rocks which cut my moccasins and made my feet bleed when I ran back and forth across them looking for the deer I had seen only a moment before."

He showed his feet with the reddened rags of his moccasins clinging to them and then, as in further proof, he untied from the thongs at his girdle some little glistening quartz-like stones such as Indians make their arrow points of. The mythkeeper laid aside his carving and took the little edged stones and turned them thoughtfully this way and that upon his palm so that they sparkled and flashed like gems in the firelight. But he did not seem to be looking at them really.

"When I was young," the mythkeeper said, "I often heard the old men talk of the white deer who was the chief of all the deer, but only twice before this, although I am now very old, have I ever met with any hunter who had seen him."

Jacques felt hungry right after that and got one of the women to give him some supper, but when he looked for the Little Chief to share it with him, he couldn't at first find him anywhere. He went on looking, however, and finally came upon him far down the slope all by himself kneeling on the ground, staring down into the embers of the signal fire they had kindled that morning. He wouldn't touch what Jacques had brought, although it was a morsel of bear liver which had been wrapped up in a bit of caul fat, spitted on a sweet-tasting hickory switch, and roasted over red coals. The Little Chief said he wasn't hungry. Jacques crouched down beside him and said between mouthfuls:

"Do you think it really was a white deer the hunter saw or do you think the sun was in his eyes?"

The Little Chief stopped him with a sudden impatient movement of his hands as though he didn't want to talk.

CHAPTER XVIII

Thanks to St. Christopher

Next morning Jacques was waked by somebody's shaking him. His mattress of deerskin and heaped dry leaves and cedar boughs was so soft, his long-haired buffalo comfort so warm, that at first he pretended he was still asleep, in the hope that the shaking would stop. But it persisted till he opened his eyes. The Little Chief was bending over him, making excited gestures. Jacques obediently got up and followed on tiptoe out between the tent-like shelters. It was barely light. Jacques was so sleepy he could hardly see where he was going. The Little Chief led the way to the spring in the ravine. There beside two piles of rolled-up skins leaned Jacques' gun. He was so surprised it waked him up.

"Are we going *hunting?*" he cried.

"Hush," whispered the Little Chief, and then, "yes."

"By ourselves, Little Chief? But won't they punish you?" Jacques by this time knew *he* would not be punished, no matter what he did. "Won't they dry-scratch you?"

The Little Chief faced him. His breath in the cold air floated off his lips like smoke from a warrior's pipe.

"I dreamed last night that I killed the white deer— I had fasted, you know," he whispered solemnly.

"Oh," said Jacques, and after a little silence: "Aren't we going to take our bows and arrows?"

"It was with your gun I killed him in my dream."

"Oh," said Jacques again. And without another word he picked up his half of the bundled skins and slung them over his back.

As they went along, the Little Chief bent down now and then to study the ground. Jacques thought he was already looking for the tracks of deer, but, when he asked, the Little Chief said he was following the trail of the returned hunter.

Toward the middle of the morning they came to a valley between two hills like high walls. At the far end they could see the way up out of the valley between two overhanging rocks. They passed through the valley, walking very slowly and watching the ridges intently, without, however, seeing there any sort of life or movement. They passed then beneath the rocks that overhung the defile and came out at the other side on a steep barren slope without any trees but covered all over with little thin-edged flaky stones that sparkled in the sun. A thin rill of water slid down past their feet. They filled their gourd cups, stirred in a little parched corn meal and drank it.

It was a beautiful morning, cold and sunny. White deer or no, Jacques thought, it was a lark to be alone together, the two of them, with the whole day before them. A little to the south across a plain ran a twisting ribbon of trees. The Little Chief thought it might be a stream course. If so there would be rocks and moss and probably deer. When they had finished eating they sprang away down the hill, the little white stones clicking and rolling under their feet, and set off toward the trees.

They found the stream, the rocks, the moss, even a well-trodden place on the bank where deer had been that very morning, but no deer. The Little Chief thought it might be a good idea to follow the stream a while. They did that. And then, remembering it was, after all, on the heights that yesterday's hunter had seen his herd, they cut across the plain farther on and explored the hills to the eastward. It seemed strange they couldn't come upon any deer at all, because again and again they found where deer had been just a little while before.

Several times Jacques wondered if he oughtn't to suggest starting for home. But then he thought of the punishment the Little Chief was almost certain to get when they should arrive, and he put it off. At last the Little Chief noticed with a start of surprise that the sun had got quite low. Then they did turn about and hurry, too. They ran for a mile or more. But twilight overtook them very suddenly in a rough hilly country and hid from them their own tracks. The Little Chief said the wisest thing was to make camp until night was past and it was light enough to find their way again.

It seemed to Jacques rather lonely at first. He remembered all the dismal stories he had ever heard of lost people. And as night came on there was a kind of howling all about that the Little Chief said was wolves. But they managed, before it was quite dark, to gather together a lot of brush on a little rocky shelf high up above the woods where the howling was. And after they got the fire lit, and, rolled up in their skins, lay sipping their cold mush and talking, it began to seem quite cheerful.

They took turns at watching and keeping the fire up. Jacques waked next morning hearing shots. He did not get wide awake instantly. But after a moment he sat up and stared about him. His gun was gone and, from the forked branch where he had hung them, his shot pouch and powder horn. The Little Chief's skin blankets lay in a huddle beyond the ashes of last night's fire. Jacques sprang up and went running down the hillside toward the firing. Two more shots cracked as he ran. He had to pass through a cedar thicket. But when he came out below it, the rest of the slope was open all the way down to the edge of a stream. The Little Chief, gun in hand, was bending over a fine russet-colored buck stretched out on the ground. Jacques gave a whoop of excitement and triumph.

The Little Chief straightened and came toward him

—slowly and with his head down. It seemed almost as if he were ashamed.

"The white one got away," he said.

Jacques gasped. He looked first at the great buck on the ground, a kill to make any hunter proud, and then he looked at his friend.

"Was there really a white one?" he said. "Are you sure?"

The Little Chief seemed unable to speak. He just shook his head. He took his knife and cut the hamstring from the deer's hindquarter and threw it away— hunters who neglected to do this were said to tire easily forever afterwards. Then he begged the deer's pardon in the customary formula. And then he sat sipping his cold mush while Jacques roasted and ate the juicy deer-tongue—it's bad luck for the hunter himself to eat of his first kill.

At last the Little Chief's spirits returned, and he told of how he had been waked in the early dawn by a deer whistling. He had sprung to his feet just in time to see, beyond the grove of cedars, a herd of deer going down to the stream in the early morning light. He had seized the gun and run, blowing the deer-call as he went. When he got to the bottom of the slope, some of the deer were already in the stream, the young bucks hooking and spurring each other playfully, splashing the water up in sprays. On the farther bank browsed tranquilly a white deer with very lofty antlers. The Little Chief loaded as fast as he could, but he wasn't fast enough— he had never practiced except with an empty gun. Before ever he got the gun against his shoulder, the white deer whistled again and bounded away into the woods, and all the herd streamed after him.

"Six shots," mourned the Little Chief. "I wasted six shots."

"You didn't *waste* the one you killed this buck with," insisted Jacques.

It seemed to him that if he could kill a buck himself, or even a doe for that matter, and of whatever color, it would make him happier than anything in the world.

"Which way did they go?" he demanded suddenly. "Let's follow—it's too early to start home anyway."

The Little Chief stared in swift admiration.

They left in such a hurry Jacques didn't finish the roasted tongue but flung it away only half eaten. They followed the stream-bed first and then crossed a broad valley and threaded a dim forest. All morning they tramped, seeing as yesterday many places where deer had been but no deer. They sat down to rest at noon and ate the last of their parched cornmeal. Moving on just afterwards, the Little Chief caught Jacques' elbow and halted him. Beyond an opening in the trees, wide and high like a church door, stretched a smooth meadow. There, nibbling at the sparse, late verdure, as peacefully as cows upon a French farm, were scattered more than a hundred deer, their warm-colored coats glossy under the sun. In the instant the boys beheld them, at the far side of the meadow, a lordly pair of antlers lifted high in air and there rang out a swift trumpeting call. The feeding deer sprang up, herded together, and bounded away after the high antlers as if following a flag, straight into the woods.

"They're coming this way," cried the Little Chief. "Quick. We can head them off if we hurry. Load the gun."

He caught the deer-call out of Jacques' hand and blew upon it. Jacques fumbled for his shot pouch as they ran.

"Give me the shot pouch," he panted.

The shot pouch, the shot pouch. Who had had it last? Had the Little Chief given it back to Jacques after he had killed the buck this morning? Had they left it in the hurry of getting started? Had they lost it on the way? What did it matter? The shot pouch was gone and the deer were coming.

Against the dark trees, shadows against shadow, the deer went by, streaming away before their eyes like meteors or phantoms.

"There," cried the Little Chief. "There. The great buck in front—wasn't he white?"

Jacques gulped and shook his head. He didn't know. Who can tell the color of a shooting star?

"Well, I guess we'd better go home now," he said after a bit. And the Little Chief nodded yes.

They plodded along sorrowfully. They had been following the tracks of capricious deer all day, and that made their trail too mixed up to follow back. So the Little Chief laid his course by the sun. But quite unexpectedly the sky grew overcast, and there was no longer any sun to go by. They tried then to pick up their trail again but couldn't. It got darker and darker —though it wasn't, it couldn't possibly be, nearly night. At last it began to snow. They were getting hungry.

Their parched meal was all gone. The Little Chief said the best thing to do was to give up trying to get home tonight and to find the way back to the deer he had killed and the safe dry ledge where they had slept the night before. But it snowed harder and harder, and they had to give that up, too, at last: it was better to go without supper than to have no fire. They gathered brush just where they were, although it wasn't an agreeable place at all but a thickly wooded hollow where you heard wolves very close about whenever you let yourself listen.

They couldn't sleep for the wolves' howling. And when daylight came again the snow made everything look different. Even the Little Chief didn't know at all where they were by that time. Jacques' feet were painfully frostbitten. They wandered this way and that, more than once crossing their own footprints in the snow. And they had nothing to eat all day but some wild garlic and onions which the Little Chief managed to grub out of the snow-covered earth with his horn spoon. They saw rabbits and beaver, too. Jacques fingered his powder horn wistfully. If only they hadn't lost the shot pouch. When it was night they made a fire and watched by turns, as before. The next day it was just the same only there were no garlic and onions. There was nothing at all. And Jacques' feet hurt so he couldn't stand.

The Little Chief stood in front of him, thinking. Suddenly he gave a whoop. His fingers flew in and out of the gewgaws at his belt. The saint's medal. The little silver saint's medal. Look. From a bit of clay dug up with a horn spoon they could make a bullet mold. They could melt the medal in the fire.

It was, in a way, as fantastic as a story about a white deer. Jacques had an idea silver wasn't good for bullets. He wasn't even sure the good God wouldn't strike you dead if you melted up a saint's image. White men have their beliefs as well as Indians. But he was too wretched to protest. He rolled himself tighter in his buffalo robes and went back to sleep. When he waked it was afternoon instead of morning and the Little Chief was standing before him holding in his palm a hard silver pellet.

"Oh—" said Jacques. And then after a silence he began again: "Only one? The little Christopher wasn't so little as to make only one, was he?"

"No. There were three. I lost the others."

"*Lost* them!"

"I thought I saw the white deer and fired—twice. It was only a cedar bush covered all over with snow. That was before noon. I have looked ever since for the two bullets. But they had buried themselves in the snow and I cannot find them."

He dropped the gun and powder horn on Jacques' knees. A black hawk poised on a gray hollow stump a little way off. Jacques inquired listlessly:

"Are black hawks good to eat?"

"They give you the accursed sickness," answered the Little Chief in the same dull tone.

"Not," declared Jacques with sudden firmness, "if killed with blessed metal."

He reached up and took the silver pellet off the Little

Chief's palm, loaded and fired. The hawk toppled down on the snow, a drop of ink on a white sheet of paper.

It was the crow that saved them—or, if you like, St. Christopher. They were both stronger after they had eaten. And the Little Chief redoubled his care in observing the sun and the way the moss grew on the tree-trunks. And the next day they found the dead deer under the snow and, on a little bush near-by, Jacques' shot pouch. After that they had no further trouble. When they came at last to the camp under the chestnut-trees, instead of being punished they were welcomed and made much of. Some of the women asked them if they hadn't been carried off by the Little People. And when the boys denied it, the women just smiled as if they didn't altogether believe them. Jacques and the Little Chief were encouraged to tell their experiences whenever other hunters told theirs around the fires at evening. And the horned man tattooed them both with a hawk and a deer on their thighs in recognition of their adventure.

CHAPTER XIX

IN THE MOON OF CROWING TURKEYS

IT was spring again. A sweet breath was in the air. The peach-trees were in bloom, pink as little dawn clouds. And at the edges of the field, where the woods began, the plum-trees showed whitened all over as if a flurry of snow had settled on them. Now and then a partridge called his gay "Bob White"—or "Hou-ouy," the Indians said. Across the brown crumbled earth moved browner figures which stooped and rose and stooped again. The work with the hoes of buffalo shoulder blades was finished. Now they were planting. The great chief was at work with the rest. You could see his feather coronal high above the others. On a scaffolding fixed between two billows of peach bloom sat the old mythkeeper in his woven white robe carving at his pipe-bowl and mildly—yet loudly, too, so that his voice should reach far across the tilled field— telling a story to entertain the people while they worked.

Jacques sat crosslegged in front of him, listening. The mythkeeper was relating the myth of the two starving hunters and the woman of heavenly beauty who appeared to them by light of the moon.

"It was the corn woman herself. Wherever her

147

feet pressed the ground the first corn sprang with its long leaves and delicate life-giving fruit."

Jacques sighed. The mythkeeper heard the sigh and leaned toward him.

"One more sun-falling and your friend will be with you again. It is not long to wait."

"No," Jacques agreed, "it's not much longer now." But he sighed again. The pipe-bowl which the myth-keeper was making had strange little faces embossed on the sides, the faces of men with the ears of animals. On the tiny stem into which the long hollow reed would be stuck later on, stood upright a little bear with uplifted paws and a man's head. "Why, you've nearly finished," exclaimed Jacques in surprise.

The mythkeeper nodded agreement. He had nearly finished. Things do come to an end, you see. He smiled at Jacques and went on with the story of the corn woman. When he came to the end, the workers in the field fell to singing all together. Jacques scrambled down from the mythkeeper's platform and walked back toward the village.

Outside the clustered houses at the end of a path stood, solitary and alone, the house in which the Little Chief was undergoing the ceremony which marked the end of his childhood. The door was a black shadow. Nothing showed beyond it. A little girl came running out of the village and set down before the door a steaming gourd cup and ran away again. A nauseous bitter odor floated from the cup. A hand came out of the door and drew the cup inside. The horned man passed the little girl on the path and approached the lonely hut on padding feet.   As he came he swished in air his whip of silk grass and the fibers of buttonsnake root stalks plaited together.   The whip tapered to a point and was knotted together at the end.   It made a smooth silky sound slashing through the air.   Jacques stepped back of a myrtleberry bush and waited.

The horned man went into the hut, and his voice began the chant that went with this part of the ceremony. But, besides the chant and the whine of the whip as it rose and fell, there was no sound at all—no outcry of pain, not even a quick gasp to stifle a cry.

When the horned man came out, Jacques was still standing there.   The horned man smiled between his painted bristles.   Jacques could not keep his eyes away from the plaited grass whip, which the horned man was looping at his belt now.   It looked wet and dark.   The horned man as though he could read Jacques' thoughts said:

"I am teaching your friend what it is good for him to know.   In the land of your birth across the great sea, do not the white fathers wish their sons taught to become brave?"

"Yes—oh, yes—but not that way, not that way at all."

The horned man stared, puzzled.   Jacques hurried away.   When he came inside the village there was no sound or movement among the houses.   Even the trodden square was empty.   It seemed strange not to hear from the alleyway beyond the town house the thump and roll of the stone discus and the shouts of the young men at their play.   A lot of the men were gone to carry the skins from the winter hunt to the French settlement. Nearly everybody else was busy at the planting. Jacques didn't see a soul as he passed through the village except a woman who was shaping a clay pot before her door. As he went by, she bent down and screened her work with her shoulder. They believed that if any but the maker looked at a pot before it was finished it would take on an ugly shape or crack when it was put over the fire.

Jacques went through the square and out between the houses at the other side. The air was full of warm sweet garden smells. Some of the Indians called this the Moon of Crowing Turkeys, because it was the month when the wild cocks sprang to the high treetops every morning and waked the world with shouting. Jacques' feet took him along the familiar path to the river. There he dropped down on the shingly bank, chose a flat pebble and shied it listlessly over the surface of the water. The Little Chief could skip a stone as many as fourteen times, but Jacques had never got his score above nine.

He chose another pebble but he checked his arm in mid-air. A little silver thread of sound quivered into the afternoon. Did his loneliness and longing make him imagine it? Or had he really heard it? He lowered his arm and listened. There it was again, thin and faint, but sweet and insistent, too, like the penetrating odor of wild plum blossoms. The little trembling tune was wordless, a mere disembodied ghost of song. But Jacques, hearing, or thinking that he heard, felt his lips begin to move:

They can talk about war
Who have never been there,
But I tell you, my friend,
It's a sorry affair. . . .

Around the curve where the current combed a stooping willow's hair came a small pirogue nosing its way upstream. In it were a naked Indian paddling and a white man seated in the stern playing a violin. The white man had on a red cloth cap which nodded in time to his bow.

"Picard!" screamed Jacques. "Picard!"

He tore off his deerskin breechclout and his belt of dangling trophies, flung himself into the water and swam downstream with all his might.

"Here, here, here," cried Picard, holding his violin high above his head. "You may be a fish nowadays, old fellow, but please remember Madame is not and never will be one."

The cheerful scolding voice made Jacques laugh aloud. He stopped where he was and contentedly trod water while Picard put the violin in its case and then in its outer swathings of tarpaulin.

"You've become quite a swimmer, haven't you?"

"Oh, so so. But how did you ever get leave to come?" begged Jacques, scrambling at last into the pirogue. "Can you stay a long time? How did you find the way?"

"A white boy in the Indian country," said Picard, answering the last question first, "is as easy to find as a church in a French village. Almost anybody can direct you."

"But wasn't it an awfully long journey?"

"It seems to me, my boy, you made the same trip once yourself."

"Oh, I came overland, not by river, and anyway I was very ill. They had to make a hammock and carry me and I didn't have any idea how long it took. It seemed months. But please tell me, how *did* you get leave?"

"Quite easily, old fellow. I was in a way invited to absent myself—"

"No, but honestly, Picard—"

"Honestly, my friend. Rations were low—practically non-existent. Indeed we hadn't been what you'd call feasting all winter. And so Monsieur de Bienville invited a few bold fellows to go junketing among the savages."

For the first time Jacques noticed how thin Picard was. His cheeks hung in folds when he laughed. And his arm, when Jacques squeezed it as they stepped ashore, felt like a dried stick inside the sleeve. Compassion pinched Jacques' heart. He knew what it was to be hungry.

"Never mind. We'll soon have you fat, Picard, fat as Monsieur Bosset. How is good Monsieur Bosset? Is he as fat as ever? Has he built his inn yet?"

"What are the—er—decorations, if I may ask?" Picard countered, pointing at Jacques' dripping thighs.

"A hawk on this leg. A deer on the other. Tattooed, you know, with a gar's-tooth comb and pitchpine soot rubbed in while it's bleeding—"

"But didn't it hurt?"

"Hurt! I should say so. I was ill a week, couldn't eat a thing but sagamité. But I wouldn't have missed having them for anything, because you see on the great hunt last winter my friend, the Little Chief—that's a sort of nickname—and I—"

"Now, old fellow, I expect to have a great deal of leisure while I'm here; and, unless you're very busy yourself, we'll have time to gossip no end. But first I'd like to get that fattening process started."

Jacques uttered a cry of self-reproach and they set off at once, leaving the Indian guide to follow with the blankets and gun and camp kettle after he should have sunk the empty pirogue to hide it, as the custom was, for the return trip. Jacques insisted on carrying the violin.

"Well, be careful of her—she's my one true love," Picard reminded.

"I know." Jacques patted the violin case as if he were caressing a woman's hand. They both laughed foolishly. "How's Marie?" asked Jacques abruptly over his shoulder. There was a little silence behind him. "Oh, I forgot. I wasn't going to ask you a single other question till you'd had something to eat."

But Picard was answering already.

"Marie is well. I brought you a letter from her. It's in my knapsack."

Halfway home they came upon the horned man sitting cross-legged on the ground gripping the gorge of a rattlesnake with his left hand and with his right applying to the snake's teeth a bit of twisted root. At the sound of their footsteps, the horned man laid the snake

gently upon the ground and spoke to it the Indian word
of farewell. As the snake slithered away in the trans-
parent shade, the horned man turned and spoke to
Jacques the greeting word.

Picard crossed himself.

"Mother of God. Is he a friend of yours?"

Jacques laughed.

"Well—a sort of friend—now. The first time we
met I thought he was going to scalp me and I fainted."

"No wonder. I'd be less afraid of the devil himself."

"How long can you stay, Picard?"

"Through the month of May, old fellow."

"The Moon of Strawberries! Oh, Picard!"

Arrived in the village Jacques put the violin carefully
down on his cane couch. And then he gathered up his
mats and skins and spread them in the sun so Picard
could rest while Jacques was getting him something to
eat. Most of the women were still in the fields. But
Jacques fetched the gourd porringer which always stood
on a bench outside the town-house door with a spoon
ready in it for the refreshment of any passing traveler.

"What's this, Jacques?"

"Hickory milk."

Picard tasted tentatively. A smile overspread his
face.

"Why, it's like rich cream!"

The buffalo horn spoon prepared for a real plunge.
Jacques caught Picard's arm, spluttering with laughter.

"Wait—wait—it's all shells at the bottom—you'll
spoil it if you stir them up."

Picard ate all he wanted. Then he shut his eyes and

lay back on the pallet.   Somewhere not far off a woman was singing her baby to sleep.   Picard asked without opening his eyes:

"Do all their women have voices like that?"

"A good many.   I think it's like mocking-birds' singing."

"Hm," murmured Picard vaguely and drifted into sleep.

Jacques rested his chin on his palms, his elbows on his knees, and let his eyes rove greedily over Picard's sleeping face.

The sun went down before Picard waked from his nap.   You could hear the voices of the people coming home from the fields, and a faint whoop as of boys playing war games far away across the prairie. Picard sat up and stretched.

"That whooping waked me," he mentioned somewhat crossly, yawning.   "Could it be us he's calling— that tall youth over yonder?"

Jacques turned in the direction of Picard's carelessly flapped hand.   The playful war whoop echoed again a little less faintly, and not far away at all, merely, in fact, at the opposite side of the trodden square.   The "tall youth" who had uttered it was running toward them in an odd inexpert fashion like a person just risen from a severe illness or a fawn new-foaled.   Midway of the square he stumbled and fell to his knees, but he quickly picked himself up again and came on, gathering strength as he came.

"Little Chief!" yelled Jacques, "Little Chief!"

CHAPTER XX

The Ladies Dance like This

There was a feast that night in Picard's honor. The women kept bringing him platters with more kinds of food than he could possibly eat. The chiefs and principal warriors gathered in from the neighboring towns and villages, and each one craved to have the guest smoke his pipe. The Little Chief, more like himself already since he had eaten a great bowl of hot smoked venison, looked on smiling from the bearskin on which he lay. Jacques, proud and happy, crouched between his two friends.

After they had eaten all they could, the red-painted pole was planted in the square. A warrior rushed forth to strike it with his war club and to chant sonorously. He began with the dawn of his manhood when he had won his glorious name He-creeps-up-and-kills and told of all the times since then—forty in all—that he had killed his man.

"What's he saying?" whispered Picard, yawning behind his hand.

"He's telling about all his exploits."

"And more," surmised Picard dropping his left eye in a droll way that made Jacques almost double up with mirth.

When the dancing began, Picard was more interested. The curious cadences seemed to challenge his ear. He got out his violin and keyed the strings. Over and over he twisted the pegs to adjust the strings and tested them with his bow, trying to coax his violin to sing in harmony with the weird music that thundered and clashed about him. But it was a French violin after all. It could play nothing but good French tunes. Picard gave up trying and was about to lay the violin back in its case when his hosts, excited by the sight of it as by some new toy, stopped their dance and came crowding about.

"They want to hear you play it," Jacques explained. Picard grinned and obligingly lifted his bow.

> On the bridge of Avignon
> They are dancing,
> They are dancing,
> The ladies dance like this,
> The ladies dance like this . . .

The familiar tune murmured gently along under the shadowy trees which only a minute before had trembled to thudding drums and whirling chichicois. A youth, tempted like Picard by a new rhythm, capered and pranced trying to keep step to Picard's music, his feather queue tossing absurdly between his shoulders, the trinkets strung from his girdle swaying and clashing against each other. Then Picard stepped out into the square and bowed to the chief's daughter, and with gestures invited her to dance. She came to him, shyly at first, and he tried to teach her the minuet.

He pinched an imagined skirt between the thumb

and forefinger of the hand that held his bow and dropped a curtsy. Then he played a strain of music and paced the measures of the dance. She did her best to imitate him. The onlookers shouted with delight. At the end of the dancing lesson Picard ran inside the hut and got from his pack a yard of brocade all shimmering white and strewn with pink rosebuds and green leaves. He presented it to the chief's daughter, bowing gallantly.

"Wear this," he said, "instead of your deerskin petticoat when you dance the minuet."

Of course she didn't understand a word he said, nor did any of the others. But they all laughed as hard as Jacques did at Picard's lavish bow and absurd gallantry. The chief's daughter made little cooing sounds of rapture and hugged the silken brocade against her breast. The chief himself in his great coronal of eagle feathers stood up in the square with his arms folded and delivered a fine oration of thanks to Picard for his generosity. And Picard presented to him on behalf of Monsieur de Bienville a beautiful scarlet coat with gold facings and gold buttons.

Between the dances Picard played love songs, and the girls crowded close and listened just as though they understood. Picard would nod at one of them and, as if he were offering her a flower, play a wisp of song— "Charming Gabrielle," perhaps, or "My Sweet Annette." And the girl he looked at would drop her eyes and dimple into smiles and coquetry. Then suddenly Picard would leap up and begin the minuet again, or the bourrée.

The Little Chief got sleepy early and slipped away. But Jacques crouched where torchlight and darkness met, and dreamed wide-eyed of ladies and gentlemen dancing the minuet under painted ceilings and crystal chandeliers. The buckles on the gentlemen's shoes twinkled as their red heels went tapping over the floor. The ladies' flowered-strewn brocades billowed about them when they curtsied low to the music.

Picard breakfasted under a pine-bough arbor on fresh-caught river trout fried in bear's oil by the chief's wife and fed to Picard as a special honor by the chief himself dressed in his fine new scarlet coat. Between the gold lapels showed strangely the chief's bare chest pricked all over with suns and moons and birds and flowers. The chief would strip a white and brown morsel of fish away from the bones and fan it this way and that to cool it, and then smiling hold it toward Picard. Picard had a droll way of opening his mouth like a baby bird gaping for worms, which made Jacques laugh aloud.

After Picard had finished his breakfast, and the chief with ceremonious dignity had taken his leave, Jacques asked Picard if he could have his letter from Marie now, and Picard went inside the hut to get it. He brought back, not one letter, but two.

"Oh—*two!* You didn't tell me there were two, Picard."

"No? Well, there are, you see. The other one came from France for you a long while ago—on the king's ship."

"The king's ship!" echoed Jacques. "You didn't tell me a ship had come."

"Hm," said Picard. He had brought his violin out, and he was tightening the strings and listening to them one by one. "Have a little patience, Jacques, my lad. There's bad news as well as good, you know."

Jacques tore open the letter from France. Though penned by hand of the priest and adorned with the pious phrases and exhortations which Aunt Gabrielle deemed a fit acknowledgment of this privilege, the letter was like a little visit home. His father and aunt were well. They missed Jacques, but otherwise they went along about as when he was there. The skipper haunted the water-front and Little Sailor Inn on the look-out for news from the New World. Aunt Gabrielle kept busy in the house and garden. The peach conserve she was making when Jacques left hadn't turned out so well. But the gooseberries were bearing nicely, and she had high hopes of a fine lot of jelly from them. They had a new cat, not such a bright pretty yellow as Susanne, but a better mouser all the same, and they were not going to spoil her as Jacques had spoiled Susanne with coddling and overfeeding. Madame Bosset was well enough, but she would fret in spite of all one could say —as though Monsieur weren't a man grown and able to look out for himself.

"Picard," said Jacques, looking up from his letter, "you haven't said one word about Monsieur Bosset. Is his inn built yet and is he making money so he can send soon for Madame?"

Even now Picard seemed to be evading him. A dew

of sweat sprang out on his upper lip and he began by telling that the king's ship—the *Pelican* it was called —all loaded down with fine white flour and sweet wines and bringing, just as Monsieur d'Iberville had promised, two dozen girls to marry the soldiers and make homes for them, had touched at the West Indies according to custom, and had taken on, unluckily, another sort of cargo.

The *Pelican* had brought yellow fever to the colony. Almost half the people had died of it—Monsieur Bosset among the first. Poor Monsieur Bosset, who was to have made a fortune and won a baronetcy and dressed Madame, his wife, all in silks like a lady. Well, he hadn't been a robust man, you know, he was not suited to a rough adventurous life. Why, he himself had said a hundred times he should never have left the Little Sailor. But his death was no less sad for all that. And the strange thing was what different sorts of men the fever took. There was Monsieur Tonti, the Iron Hand. You would scarcely have thought that, after all the dangers he'd been through, he'd die in his bed like any plump little inn-keeper, now would you? Yet the fever carried him off. There was yet more of the unhappy news. Monsieur d'Iberville was ill in France and unable to come in the *Pelican* to visit his colony. And as to Monsieur de Bienville, a young man barely grown and governor of a colony where troubles sprouted like seed corn—*his* lot was no boy's game, you may be sure. Did Jacques remember the royal commissary?

"Monsieur Nicolas?" cried Jacques with a short

laugh. "How could I forget him and his dirty purple plume?"

Well, Monsieur Nicolas was becoming more powerful all the time now. The *Pelican* had brought along a number to take his part; and Monsieur Nicolas had actually won over the new priest.

"Oh, that Monsieur Nicolas will make a peck of trouble for our young governor, as sure as Madame here is my wife. But aren't you going to read Marie's letter, old fellow?"

Jacques broke the seal.

"What's the trouble?" Picard demanded after a bit.

"Why," hesitated Jacques, "it doesn't sound as if Marie wrote it."

"Well, she didn't, as a matter of fact, you know."

"Oh, I know *that*. But she must have told the priest what to write down—she made her mark at the end of it— and it doesn't sound a bit like Marie. It's so—" he searched for a word—"solemn."

"Marie's not particularly merry these days, Jacques."

"It's that Pierre Coudret," Jacques guessed sadly. And Picard nodded. "Is Marie really his wife, Picard?"

"His lawful wife. He'd quarreled with her in France, you know, and run away here to the New World. He didn't like her following him and wasn't any too ready to make it up, I guess. But Monsieur de Bienville patched things up between them somehow and got him to agree to build a house for her. It took him a long time to build it. I had to put the roof on, myself." Picard's voice was grim. "Well, after that, things seemed to be going along fairly well for a time. They set up housekeeping. Monsieur de Bienville gave them one of the cows that came on the *Pelican*. One saw Marie going to church—"

"Church!" Jacques exclaimed. "You didn't tell me we had a church!"

Picard ignored the interruption.

"One saw her going to church," he repeated, "of a Sunday morning like any contented peasant woman leaning on her good man's arm in her clean white kerchief and cap. But after a bit this precious husband of hers made off again—where, nobody rightly knows. But some of the soldiers say they've seen him in the Indian villages up-country, naked and painted all over like one of their warriors, with his ears cut and stretched as big as hoops and his red hair done up in colored feathers—the woodpecker!"

"What will poor Marie do now?"

"Go on watching the river for pirogues, I guess," said Picard with a wry face as though the words were sour on his tongue. Then suddenly the old familiar grin stole over his lean face. His eyes crinkled up at the corners. He asked in the manner of introducing a cheerful even a merry subject: "I haven't told you how close I came to being a married man, have I?"

"No," said Jacques with a swift wistful smile. "Tell me."

"Do you remember a tall Gascon with a stoop who was so shy that when he started to speak he always stammered? Well, as soon as the *Pelican* got in with all the girls aboard, this chap was crazy to get married, but it was like he couldn't make up his mind which one to court. It seems he made the mistake of consulting one of the other soldiers, and the story got about. And soon everybody was after him morning and night pretending they wanted to help him decide. They picked out the two prettiest, and some would try to persuade him to go after the blonde, and the others would talk up the brunette. The little dark one—her name was Annette—was gobbled up by one of the Canadians right away, and the next day Manon, the fair one, married, too. The soldiers urged other candidates on the Gascon, always two at a time, to keep him undecided. Well, would you believe me, while the lout was still hemming and hawing, all of the girls got married but one.

"However, he went to call on *her* at last and it seemed he'd really got his courting started. But still those rascally soldiers pestered him like so many mosquitoes, telling him there'd be another shipment soon and perhaps he'd better not marry before it came. So he'd go to see this left-over girl, and then he'd come back to the barracks and sit and think, looking worried. One night there'd been a lot of drinking—this was while there was still plenty of the wine and brandy the *Pelican* had brought—and some of the soldiers got around the Gascon and said they were going to help him make up his mind that night. And, before I knew what was happening, he and I were playing a game of cards to see which of us should have this left-over girl—"

"And you lost," cried Jacques.

"Lost! I? Ah, but you see this wasn't one of the

pretty ones at all. The fact is, she looked more like a guardsman than a girl. That's how she came to be left over so long. No, old fellow, it was the Gascon who lost."

While Jacques was still laughing, the Little Chief came running toward them. Picard went into the hut and brought out his gun and handed it to the Little Chief.

"Tell him it's a present," Picard said to Jacques. "Tell him I hope he'll kill a lot of squirrels and rabbits with it."

And before Jacques could speak a single word, he seized his violin and walked away, fiddling as he went. Good old Picard. Jacques repeated Picard's words to the Little Chief and saw his eyes widen incredulously.

"He gives it to me? Your friend gives me his own gun?"

And the Little Chief began at once to plan all he would do with Picard's gun. He would kill more deer and buffalo in the great hunt next winter than any boy in the tribe. Jacques smiled dreamily. He hardly listened to the Little Chief.

From the cornfield far away rolled the voice of the mythkeeper, mild and sonorous, recounting some old beloved legend to the people while they planted. Vibrating oddly through that rolling sound went Picard's violin growing fainter and fainter until at last it became as unsubstantial as a dream. Close by, a woman was pounding corn and singing to her baby. The woman's song wasn't like a French song at all. It was more like the way birds sing, just a few notes repeated over and

over, but achingly sweet and full of little trills like
water trembling in the sun.

Is it boy or girl, ball-sticks or bread?
The wren flies low and is half afraid.
When a boy is born,
The birds are sad:
"Ah, me!   Ah, me!
His arrows sting."
His arrows sting,
When a girl is born,
The birds are glad:
"Oh, thanks!   Oh, thanks!
She'll grind sweet corn,
She'll grind sweet corn."

Gulf wind, blow
Her cradle slow—
   Loo-loo-loo.
Mocking-bird, sing.
A girl child swings—
   Loo-loo-loo.

Is it boy or girl, is it bow or meal?
Nearer and nearer the crickets steal.
When a boy is born,
The cricket's sad:
"Ah, me!   Ah, me!
He'll kill, I know,
He'll kill, I know."
When a girl is born,
The cricket's glad:
"Oh, thanks!   Oh, thanks!
I'll sing her a song,
I'll sing her a song."

Jacques heard the Indian lullaby just as he heard the
Little Chief's voice close beside him, but he wasn't really

listening to either one.   He lay with his hands clasped under his head and looked through half-closed eyes at the bud-misted branches overhead.   His thoughts, set going by Picard's news, went far away.   They wandered now about the streets of a certain walled town in France, now about a tiny log fort clinging to the hem of the New World.

"And I shall win my war name with your friend's gun, too," said the Little Chief.

Jacques sat bolt upright.

"There isn't any war," he said sharply.   "All the chiefs and warriors smoked the calumet with the French a year ago.   There hasn't been a fresh scalp hung on the scalp-poles since I came here.   Only last week the hunters set off through the heart of the enemy country to carry skins to the French settlement—"

"There is no war now.   But there will be war again. There *has* to be," said the Little Chief smiling at Jacques.   "How else could the young men get names for themselves?"

CHAPTER XXI

The News Whoop

That year, Jacques' second among the Indians, went faster than the first. Picard's visit, to begin with, was over in a flash—although he stayed, as promised, till the prairies were painted red all over with strawberries. The young corn grew, and the Green-eared Moon came almost before Jacques knew it. During the fete he and the Little Chief joined a party of young men for a visit down through the towns in the one-time enemy nation. There was feasting and dancing and singing in every public square they came to. And then it seemed they were hardly home again before it was autumn and the air was chilly and full of the smell of burning. The persimmons were so plentiful that fall that the whole village moved in a body far down into the southward woods to harvest them. Jacques and the Little Chief chased turkeys, opossums, raccoons, in such long forays from the woodland camp that sometimes they didn't get back till the next day. And once with some deer-hunters they went again down into the lower nation—though only among the upper towns this time, because it was almost time for the winter hunt by then.

And now even the great hunt was over. The village hummed with excitement. They were making ready the hunters' spoils to carry down to the French settlement. More than half the people were going. It would be a gay junket. For it followed the luckiest winter hunt ever recorded on the notched sticks and bead chaplets of the mythkeeper, and ahead were the fabulous wonders of the white men's town. The Little Chief was going. Jacques was not. He felt a little wistful watching all the preparations.

The women packed the smoked venison into their corn-carriers; tightened the loops on the balloon-like deerskin bags of bear oil; and packed the deer and buffalo hides—hundreds and hundreds of them—into bales. The skins of Jacques' kill were in the bales; seven deer and two buffalo—nothing to compare of course with the twenty deer and eight buffalo which the Little Chief had brought down with Picard's gun, but a respectable number all the same. Jacques was proud of his skins. He reminded the Little Chief several times to be sure to show them to Picard before trading them in for powder and shot as agreed. Skins were just the same as money at the French fort. One skin, for instance, would buy at the king's warehouse two little horn-handled knives, or four balls of shot worth ten sous.

The Little Chief and Jacques made a bundle of broken sticks, such as the warriors used for reckoning time till the day for setting out to war or for keeping any other important engagement. Jacques, beginning when the Little Chief left, was to throw away one stick every day. In this way he would be able to follow the whole journey with fair accuracy.

The first stage of that journey they both knew almost

mile by mile. They drew with a stick in the ashes a map of the country with every creek and swamp as clear as print upon it. They knew how long it should take the Little Chief to get to the salt lick where they had watched together all night for deer; just how long to the creek that marked the southern boundary of this nation; and so on down to where the towns of the next nation began and then to where they ended. They didn't know how many sticks to allow for the part from there to Fort Louis. But some of the men who had made the trip before helped them to calculate that last lap of the journey, too. The men said they would stay a week at Fort Louis: seven sticks for that. And of course it would take as long to come back as to go. The bundle of broken twigs, representing each a lonely day for Jacques, was, at last, as big around as his arm. He couldn't help sighing as he pushed it down into the skin wallet he wore tied to his girdle. He promised the Little Chief faithfully he would throw away a stick every day until the Little Chief got back.

Jacques gave the Little Chief "talking leaves" which the Little Chief handled reverently and stowed in a special otter-skin purse like some sort of sacred charm. The letter was addressed to Picard. It asked him to get the master cannoneer to show the Little Chief exactly how the fire-belching cannon were set off, and please to ask the skipper of whatever sloop should chance to be lying in the river to show him all about sails and rigging and such.

The day before the great journey the Little Chief in solemn ecstasy made his final preparations. He had

had the outer cartilage of his ears cut and stretched with wires so that they stood out from his head in great hoops like the young warriors'. He dressed his hair with fresh bear's oil and a bright new blue jay's wing. He added a fox brush painted scarlet to his trophy belt. He spent hours and hours before a little French mirror painting suns and moons and stars on his breast. His joy assumed such proportions at the last that he was unable to talk. He just listened with burning eyes to all the instructions Jacques gave him and nodded dumbly. In the end when he came running up, jingling and glittering in all his finery, to say good-by, he could fetch from his swelling painted chest no more than a single strangled, "I go," as he gripped Jacques' hand and squeezed it till it hurt.

Jacques wouldn't have had the Little Chief miss going to the fort. But after he had left, things were very dull. The first week was bad enough. There was hardly anything to eat: all the smoked meat had been carried away to be bartered for knives and garter bells and vermilion. There was nothing left in the village but a bit of dried squash and parched meal. And then it set in to rain and kept it up day after day.

Jacques lay on a bench against the wall of the town house and listened to the winter rain drumming on the thatched roof. It was still afternoon but inside it was as dark as night. The cane mats, hung over the door to keep out the rain and cold, shut out, too, what little light there was. The air, besides, was blue with smoke of lightwood knots and of the old men's pipes. Jacques yawned and sat up. He tightened his belt to try to

ease his hunger.   Then he fumbled in the skin pouch
hanging against his naked thigh and drew out his bundle
of broken sticks.   He untied the wisp of twisted bark
with which they were bound together, took one stick
out, tossed it toward the fire, tied up the rest and returned them to his pouch.   According to the count of
the sticks, the Little Chief was at the French fort now.
Jacques wondered what he was doing.

A baby born yesterday wailed, got choked and held
its breath as if it would never go on.   From the faces
of the women you couldn't have told which one it belonged to.   Nobody paid any attention to it.   Two of
the women were playing a game like dice with persimmon stones painted black on one side and red on the
other.   The rest were listening to the mythkeeper, who
was midway of the story of the Nameless Young Man:
"Once more the pipe of war with its red and black feathers passed from hand to hand among the chiefs and old
wise men.   The great chief dealt out to the warriors
the bundles of broken sticks to reckon the days till it
was time to go.   The last bundle of all he gave to the
nameless young man.   The young man's parents re-
joiced that at last their son was going out to war to get
a man's name for himself, and the maiden who loved
him wept with pride and joy. . . ."

Jacques had heard the old story so many times by
now that he knew it by heart.   He was no longer stirred
to hear of the youth who was to die at last without the
name he coveted.   He hardly listened as the mythkeeper neared the end of the mournful story.   He took
out of his pouch a little flint-tipped tool and a chunk

of redstone, moved nearer to the fire, squatted down, and began to chip tiny flakes of stone off on the ground.

Looking up when the voice of the mythkeeper stopped, Jacques saw that the eyes of the chief's daughter were filled with tears. He looked at her curiously. Why should the familiar old tale suddenly move her like that? She was nearly grown now and very beautiful. She had a blue French ribbon plaited in her shiny black hair. She met Jacques' eyes and smiled through her tears. She leaned a little toward him and touched the chunk of redstone on his palm.

"You are making a warrior's pipe?" Yes, he was making a pipe. "For . . . " she hesitated and when the word came it was almost as though she caressed it, too, with her finger-tips " . . . the Little Chief?"

"No! What would he do with a warrior's pipe? He's nothing but a boy."

She seemed amused. She smiled to herself as at some delicious secret. All she said was:

"The Little Chief is growing very fast. And it takes more than a day to carve a pipe."

Jacques flung the stone chunk from him as hard as he could. It struck the heart of the fire. A shower of sparks flew up and scattered all over the bearskins on which the old men were lying. The old men had to brush the sparks away with their gnarled brown fingers. Jacques stammered an apology. Then he stared at the chief's daughter. There was all about him an emptiness he couldn't at first account for.

"Why, it's stopped raining," he discovered at last.

"Yes," said the chief's daughter.

And she smiled again. She went and lifted down the cane mats hanging before the door. The air outside was burnished copper. Pools of water in the square mirrored painted clouds. Between the pools, two little boys were walking about on their hands, their naked bodies gleaming. A girl child who had lost her first tooth was running around and around waving her clenched fist with the tooth inside and shrilling:

"Beaver, beaver, put a new tooth in my jaw!"

"Why don't you get a squirrel or a rabbit before the light goes?" said the chief's daughter over her shoulder to Jacques. "There is much dry fuel in my father's house. I will cook your kill for you."

Jacques' French gun was useless of course until the Little Chief should get back with some powder and shot. So he took his blowgun instead and went out. The clean cold air bathed all his body. He forgot about being annoyed as he sprang into that long, loping stride the Little Chief had taught him.

He soon found a rabbit. It was scurrying toward the thickets that fringed the open prairie. The rabbit stopped when Jacques stopped, as though by standing immovable it could persuade him it was only a bit of stubble and not a rabbit at all. It didn't turn its head but stared sideways out of one eye in the way that rabbits have. Jacques felt a stir of compunction. He'd been pretty lucky to kill seven deer and two buffalo on the winter hunt. It seemed as though he ought perhaps to let the rabbit off. It looked very small and soft with no defense but its foolish ruse. But then Jacques

thought of the fire the chief's daughter was already
kindling, and remembered how rabbit smells roasting.
A spasm of pure hunger pinched his stomach.   He fitted
an arrow grimly into his blowgun, put his lips to the
opening, aimed, and blew hard.

Going home at last, the rabbit dangling limply down
his bare leg, he heard a whoop.   He stopped and
listened.   Northward over the prairie the sister villages and towns of the nation stretched away like a great
circling slice of barbecued pumpkin.   The evening fires
were golden in the dusk, and the drums were calling tum-
tum-tum.   Through the distant pounding, the whoop
sounded again.   It was nearer that time.   It was what
they called the news whoop.   It seemed to come from
the next village.   Jacques recalled that a party from that
village had passed in the early morning going out to
hunt with guns and a deer-head decoy.   He hadn't
seen them come back.   But maybe they were back.
Maybe they had had a good kill in spite of rain and
were sending word to their neighbors that there would
be feasting and dancing in their town-house to-night.   It
would be nice if the news whoop meant that something
gay and exciting was about to happen.   Venison was better to eat than rabbit.   Jacques raced home as fast as
he could go.   But as he ran a little uneasiness nibbled
at his mind.   What if the hunters returning from the
woods to the south had brought home bad news of some
sort?   It was a long way to Fort Louis.   What if the
Little Chief's party had not got there yet after all?
What if they had met with some mishap along the
road?

CHAPTER XXII

Monsieur de Bienville

Monsieur de Bienville sat in the government house at Fort Louis writing a letter to the king's minister: "I take the liberty, Monseigneur, to render account to your highness of the state in which the colony finds itself at present. The soldiers are nearly naked. We need flour and lard and wine. Unless a ship comes soon we shall all be eating mast in the woods with the hogs. But, whatever our difficulties, I am happy to say that the two great Indian peoples north of us, between whom my brother the Sieur d'Iberville concluded peace, continue still at amity toward each other and toward ourselves. As I write, we furnish entertainment and hospitality to a great party from the farther of the two nations, come without constraint to trade and make holiday among us. . . ."

When he came to the end of the page, Monsieur de Bienville slipped the unfinished letter into his writing-case, took down his greatcoat from a peg in the log wall and went out, cramming his arms in his sleeves as he went.

The open space about the log fort presented a cheerful sight. Across it a half-dozen campfires blazed and crackled in the late afternoon. Among them moved

tlement.   A few more minutes of listening and waiting
and a runner bounded among them—one of the Indian
party who had been out hunting.   A lot of small game
swung at his thighs.   His shoulders shone with sweat.
There was no guessing how many miles he had run.
The warriors were already gathered in at one fire to
receive him.   He sprang among them crying his news:

"War," he panted, "war."   His naked, sweat-pol-
ished arm swept a half circle northward.   "Our enemies
have reddened their arrows against us.   I have read
their message on a tree."

A woman began to wail.   Children and other women
raised a dismal echo.   Somebody upset a cooking-pot.
It doused the flames it stood on, and foul-smelling smoke
rolled off in choking clouds.   The horned magician rose
in the midst of the warriors.   He held a bleached buf-
falo-shoulder blade slanting downward toward the fire
and read from it as from a parchment scroll:

"We are cut off from the land of our fathers and
from all our kindred. . . . "

Monsieur de Bienville turned sharply back into the
thickening dusk and hastened into the fort.

Crossing the parade ground he all but collided with
two men so deep in conversation they failed to see him
coming.   They started apart when they recognized
him and greeted him with self-conscious effusiveness.
Monsieur Nicolas, the royal commissary, caught off
his hat and almost brushed the ground with its purple
plume.   The priest's forefinger and thumb stroked
at the cord which girdled his black robe as he murmured
in a silky voice:

"Ah, it is Monsieur de Bienville.   Good evening,

Monsieur.   A bit of real winter we're having at last, Monsieur."

Monsieur de Bienville replied to their greetings dryly and turned to beckon a passing soldier.

"Take a message to Major Boisbriant," he rapped out.   "Ask him to see me at once in the government house.   Then find Picard, the carpenter—he was in Place Royale a moment ago—and tell him I want him."

There was a fire on the hearth in the government house.   A black boy crouching beside it got up grinning and fawning.

"Get some more wood," the governor ordered.   "I may be busy here till midnight."

The black boy slid out through the door.   Monsieur de Bienville hung up his greatcoat and dropped down at the hewn pine table.   His writing-case lay before him.   He opened it and took out the letter he had begun that afternoon to the king's minister.   Holding the pages down in the firelight he read what he had written.   When he came to the part about the Indians —the one bit of good news the letter contained—he laughed grimly and tossed that sheet into the fire. There was a knock at the door.   He called, "Come in," and Major Boisbriant appeared on the threshold.

"You sent for me, Bienville?"

The young governor made a small gesture toward the hubbub outside the fort.

"One of their hunters has just come in with a rumor—"

"I know.   I heard."

"If it's true, of course, they're really cut off from

home. And it was we who persuaded them they could safely come and go through the country of their enemies."

"Then I'd better march up with them."

"A dangerous job, I'm afraid."

Major Boisbriant shrugged slightly. A red log on the hearth crumbled and fell apart. A flame like a whispered sigh went up from it. Picard the carpenter came in and closed the door behind him. He carried his violin and bow in his left hand. With his right he doffed his red cloth cap. He had evidently come on the run. He was breathing hard.

"You wanted me, Messieurs?"

"Yes, Picard," said Monsieur de Bienville. "I want you to show Major Boisbriant on this map which village young Duval is in."

Picard came close to the table, laid down his things and bent over the rude map, squinting to see it in the firelight.

"I cannot read the names. If you will kindly show me where our fort is, Monsieur—" Monsieur de Bienville laid a finger on the map. Picard set his own carefully beside it. "Ah." Picard's finger traveled slowly upriver, turned inland, stopped. "There. There is his village." He straightened and looked from one to the other of the two officers. "Is Jacques Duval in any danger, Messieurs?" They made no answer. Picard cried: "If he is, Messieurs, please permit me to go to him. The rivers are up now. I can get through very quickly."

Monsieur de Bienville answered calmly:

"Major Boisbriant is starting to-morrow to escort our Indian guests home. If he gets through he will bring Duval back with him."

Picard grew excited. His voice rose.

"But even if Major Boisbriant gets through it will take him weeks, going overland. I can get there by water in half the time, Monsieur, traveling by night and hiding by day——"

"That will do, Picard." Monsieur de Bienville's lips set in a firm line. "Every man not included in Major Boisbriant's escort will be needed here."

Picard stared blankly. Major Boisbriant smiled at him.

"Travel to the north just now is not without danger, Picard, as you seem to understand," said the Major. "You really can't expect Monsieur de Bienville to——er ——put all his eggs in one basket, now can you?"

Picard shook his head and seizing his cap and violin stammered:

"Then good-night, Messieurs."

"Good-night, Picard."

Monsieur de Bienville cleared his throat.

"How many men shall you require, Boisbriant?"

"Oh . . . twenty-five. It hardly matters. If I took the whole garrison it wouldn't be enough." Major Boisbriant took up his hat and put out his hand to his friend. "I'll go and tell the Indians they're to have a guard. Maybe that will quiet them. And then I'll turn in and get a good night's rest before starting, I think. Good-night, Bienville."

"Good-night, my friend."

Left alone Monsieur de Bienville drew a fresh sheet of paper toward him and took up his pen. He wrote: "There is war again between the Indians north of us. The Spaniards are not so friendly as they were at first. I expect trouble in that quarter. With regard to the charges which I understand are to be preferred against my honor by the curate and the commissary, I can only say, Monseigneur, that they are false. The commissary is a parsimonious and vindictive man who thinks less of the advancement of this colony than of its destruction; and as to the priest—"

An impatient exclamation broke from his lips and he glanced toward the hearth, frowning. Why didn't that black boy come along with the lightwood knots? The fire was almost dead now and the room was full of shadows. Monsieur de Bienville's hand shook with cold. He got up, lit a lumpy homemade candle from the embers on the hearth, took down his greatcoat from the wall, wrapped it about his shoulders and sat down. But he did not take up his pen again.

The map of the Gulf Coast country, rudely drawn and full of errors, still lay spread before him under the guttering myrtle-berry candle. What a fantastic thing that anyone should have attempted to chart with black lines on white paper such vast dim forests, such mysteries of winding river, such strange and secret villages . . . equally futile of course to set down his own bitter struggles for a courtier with lace at his wrists to read yawning in a damask-cushioned chair.

He swept the still unfinished letter back into his writing-case again, blew out the candle and went out. He said good-night to the sentry outside the gate of the fort.   Place Royale was quiet at last.   The Indian warriors still sat in solemn conclave.   But the women and children were asleep in their skin rugs.   Monsieur de Bienville walked out to the edge of the bluff.   The warriors' fire spread a somber glow on the black chasm where the river ran.   The sound of oars licked at the darkness.   A pirogue pointing upstream slid into the patch of light and out again.   Two Indians were paddling.   The reflected blaze glinted transiently on their dark skins as the pirogue crossed the light.   The white face of the third man in the pirogue was an indistinguishable blur but he unmistakably wore a red cap.   Monsieur de Bienville turned sharply and opened his mouth to call the sentry.   But then a weariness fell on him and he kept silent.   What if the carpenter did risk his life on a fool's errand?   Weren't they all, perhaps, doing the same?

CHAPTER XXIII

The Black Drink

WHEN Jacques got home with his rabbit, the courier whose whoop he had heard was already shut up in the chief's house with the old men.   There was no use asking the women what the news was.   They didn't know any more than Jacques did.   The chief's daughter had a bright fire going out in the square, and the water in her earthern pot was beginning to boil.   Jacques handed her the rabbit and squatted down to warm himself by the fire.   From the chief's house sounded the voices of the old men, an indistinguishable rumble.   The news couldn't have been anything very exciting, good or bad, Jacques guessed, to call forth so many long dull speeches. "Just some more of their politics," he concluded.   And as soon as his rabbit, nicely dressed and spitted on a stick, began to fry and splutter fragrantly over the fire, he forgot the whole business.   After he had eaten, he went back to the town-house and curled up in his bearskin for the night.   Some of the women were dancing around the fire in the middle of the big room, but Jacques fell asleep at once.

When he waked some while later, the town-house was full of men—not only the old men, who alone remained now in this village, but many visiting chiefs and warriors besides. Their faces were nearly all vaguely familiar. Jacques, viewing them drowsily through the smoke-filled air, thought there must be a delegation from every town and village of the nation. They had evidently sent away the women who had been dancing and taken over the town-house for their meeting. Evidently, too, they had overlooked Jacques asleep on his bench in the shadows against the wall. If they should notice him now, they would be sure to hustle him up out of his warm skins and outdoors into the cold. He took care to lie still and keep the bearskin down over his face.

He remembered the news whoop he had heard in the late afternoon and wondered if he were going to learn anything about it now. Perhaps not. Perhaps the warriors were only recounting in that fanciful way of theirs the tale of their adventures. One never knew whether the story had to do with yesterday or a decade ago. And yet the warrior who was talking now was, Jacques saw by peeping out of his bearskin, one who had gone that morning out to hunt.

"I knew well," said the warrior, "a certain salt lick where always I find deer. I settled my antlered decoy upon my shoulder pack and turned aside from my fellows. As I bounded through the trees watchful for any rattlesnake that might lie coiled near my path, I came suddenly, not on a rattlesnake, surely, but upon his deadly trail. On a tree full before my eyes was the death message posted."

The speaker paused. Jacques did not understand. But in a moment the voice went on:

"There on the tree where the bark had been slashed

away was the picture of a warrior with lifted head-breaker and of a fleeing woman whose hair floated on the wind behind her. Beneath the picture, fastened to the tree-trunk, a reddened arrow pointed to our villages." So it was just an old story. There was no war now. Jacques was dozing off when the vigorous voice of the warrior roused him again. "I flung away my hunting pack with the treasured deer-head mask I had been more than two moons in fashioning. I sped homeward sounding the news whoop as I ran. Even now my muscles tingle with the speed of my running."

Even now! Jacques blinked. But that would mean it had just happened. He peeped cautiously out of his bearskin. The warrior stood close by the fire. Its light struck upward over his craggy cheek-bones and threw the shadow of his crest of black hawk feathers up the wall to the ceiling. He held in his hand an arrow. And he lifted it up so that everyone could see it. It was painted red. It had a lock of woman's hair trail, ing down from it. Only a few hours ago, somewhere in the familiar southward woods, this man had found that painted arrow, the sign of war!

Moreover, the pipe they were passing from hand to hand and puffing in turn had a stem sheathed in the neck feathers of the carrion crow, glossy and black. Its tufts and aigrettes were black, too, and its down-sweeping fan was made of red flamingo feathers. It was the great pipe of war. Jacques recognized it at once. He had seen it often in the house like a temple where the people kept their valued things. But he had never seen them smoking it before.

"It was the white men," the orator declared, "who persuaded us to be at peace with our ancient foe in the southward country. Now whose part will the white men take—the enemy's or ours? Did our kindred marching so happily down to the French town to trade their skins for tinkling bells and little trinkets walk into an ambush there? Perhaps the French did not really want their deer and buffalo skins at all, but their scalps instead, to send over the ocean to their great chief to hang on his scalp-poles—" No, no, Jacques wanted to cry aloud. No matter which side the French take, they wouldn't do that! But he did not make a sound. He pressed his fists against his mouth and lay rigid. "They sent a white boy here to live among us. Was that, indeed, as they declared, for the purpose that the white men and we might in time talk together, brothers at one burning fire, telling each the other the old beloved legends of our peoples? Or is that boy really a spy sent to learn how our towns and villages lie across the Strawberry Plain so that the white warriors may one day the more easily attack us?"

On and on they talked. When they had all smoked, they brewed a great foaming pot of the black drink and sat solemnly sipping it while the speakers one after another held forth. Jacques kept hoping they would say right out what they were going to do with him. And he wished with all his heart that they would make some plan for sending an armed party out to bring the Little Chief and the other travelers safely home, or at least a messenger down the river to Fort Louis to warn them not to start back until there was peace once more.

But nothing of the sort was mentioned. Many of the speeches, as the tedious custom was, did not even relate to the present crisis at all, but to past wars with their old enemy. Worn out with listening, Jacques fell asleep at last.

When he waked again, somebody was shaking him. It was quiet in the town-house now, and dark. Dim figures lay on every bench. The hot air was full of smoke and the smell of steamy bodies. One of the women was standing by him holding out a traveler's pack and a little skin meal bag.

"Am I going somewhere?" Jacques asked wonderingly.

She shook her head to show she knew no more about it than he did. But she still held out the things. So he took them and flung his feet to the ground, yawning. He glanced at his gun hanging on the wall, but it was no good of course without powder or shot. He took down instead his quiver of arrows and his black locust wood bow. He tied the meal bag to his belt, slung the sleeping-rugs and bow and quiver at his shoulder, and followed the woman out, yawning still and rubbing his eyes.

A knot of men stood waiting in the wan, early light. Jacques looked from one to the other of them. He saw the warrior with the black hawk feather crest who had said last night that Jacques might be a spy. He recognized all the others, too, vaguely, as men from the neighboring villages who had been at the council last night, but he did not know even the name of a single one of them. Although they were all of this same nation, they seemed more like strangers than friends. They fell silently into line as he came out, and the man with the black hawk feathers signed to Jacques to take his place midway among them.   Jacques would have liked to ask where he was going.

North ran the circling line of sister villages.   At first he thought maybe the men were taking him home with them so they could watch over him and decide whether he really was a spy or not.   But then he knew right away that that guess was wrong—you don't need a roll of sleeping-skins and a meal bag to go from town to town across the friendly prairie.   South stretched the plains and woods that were so full of danger now, but that, all the same, was the way to Fort Louis where the Little Chief and all Jacques' other friends were.   And at least Jacques knew the country down that way.   He would have faced south willingly enough, taking his chance at the danger.   East was the way to the river.   You could get down to Fort Louis that way, too, now that the waters were up.   It wouldn't be any safer, maybe, than the overland way, but it would be quicker. . . .

It was west they went.   All Jacques knew of the country ahead was that there wasn't a single white men's settlement in that direction, just the vast dim continent reaching on and on, wilderness upon wilderness.   Why were they taking him west?   Ahead across the rolling prairie, the sky was rosy with reflected dawn.   Behind them in the square one of the old men was calling the children up for their morning swim.   Jacques could hear them waking with the noise of a treeful of birds.

CHAPTER XXIV

The Shadow Bridge

THE men who were taking Jacques away had scarcely lost sight of their own villages across the humped plain when they began to travel with extreme secrecy. They lifted their feet high so as not to trample the tall brown prairie grass and each stepped exactly in the tracks of the one ahead so that the whole line should leave the trail of but one man. Jacques, midway of the line, was expected to do the same, of course. When they had to cross any woods, one stood behind a tree and kept a sharp look-out in every direction till the whole line had got by. Sometimes they stopped to let somebody climb a tall tree and survey the surrounding country. If they came to a tree that had been blown down, they walked along it as on a foot-log, so that even that single trail on the ground should disappear entirely for a space. In the river bottoms, which were all afloat on account of the recent rains, they waded—or swam if necessary—and that, of course, left no track at all. When they had to speak, they did it in monosyllables, whispered, as though the leaves on the trees had ears.

It was the usual mode of travel in time of war, as Jacques knew from war games with the Little Chief and his companions. But it got on his nerves all the same. Once he started and almost cried out when a dead limb snapped in the oppressive quiet and crashed to the ground behind them. And once, when the man with the crest of black-hawk feathers—the one who had said Jacques might be a spy—touched him from behind to remind him to step up on a "hurricane tree," Jacques really did cry out. The sound of his own voice, breaking out startled in the silent, secret woods, made a sweat burst out upon him. He was as wet as if they had just swum a river.

At the first stop for rest they gave Jacques a skin water-bag and sent him down a hill to a spring for water. It was such a relief to him to be alone for a little that he made the errand last as long as possible. Before he filled the water-bag, he lay on his stomach and drank deeply from the spring and then he dashed the cold clear water over his hot cheeks and forehead. Then he squatted back on his heels and took out of the pouch at his thigh the dwindled bundle of broken sticks and threw one away as he had done religiously every single day since the Little Chief had left. Before he tied up the remaining sticks to return to the pouch he counted them carefully, twice over. The sticks were more than half gone.

The Little Chief was due to be starting home. Maybe he had already started—a day this way or that must be allowed for. The thought made Jacques' heart stand still. He could see the party walking, in gay holiday humor, all happy and unsuspecting, straight toward the country of the enemy. But surely at the fort they would have heard the news of war. They would wait

HE THREW A STICK AWAY.

till there was peace again.   Or even if they had started
they would find war signs on the trees and turn back.
And yet as he climbed the hill with the water-bag he
found himself making calculations.   How far beyond
the enemy country was Fort Louis?   How many broken
sticks had the men told him and the Little Chief to allow
for that southern stage of the journey?   How many
days, in short, would it take any who might be traveling
up from Fort Louis to reach the first of the enemy
towns?   If somebody set out southward now from here,
would he have time to circle the enemy towns and come
out on the trail below to head off the northward travelers?   It would, he reckoned, be a thing just possible.
He even toyed a little with the idea that it might be
possible, too, to slip away—after dark.   But he checked
himself: he was hardly so foolish as to believe he could
run away from Indians.   Even if he should be lucky
enough to get a whole night's start of them, his trail
would be as plain as print to them by daylight, and no
matter how well he ran they would gain on him surely
and overtake him at last.

When he reached the hilltop with his water-bag, they
all ate their meal-and-water gruel, tightened their belts,
and took up the march again.   Every step was carrying
Jacques farther away from the Little Chief.   As the
Little Chief drew nearer home—if he really had started
—mile for mile Jacques was getting farther away.   They
had been traveling since daylight and it was afternoon
now.   He kept looking at the sun.   They were running straight into it.   They swam creeks, they crossed
canebrakes, they mounted hills, but always they headed

west, bounding along as though they were racing with the sun for the horizon.

In the late afternoon they topped a rise looking down on a heavily wooded valley which lay exactly in their course. The trees in the valley ahead, although leafless, were so close together that the tops seen from above were like a thick gray carpet you could walk on. Out of that impenetrable wood floated up a thin blue cloud of smoke. A wave of hesitation went through the running file of men. They slackened their pace and halted, looking at each other. Then without a word the leader turned sharply at right angles. Instead of going down into the valley he led them at an increased speed northward along the ridge.

Hope burst like a rocket in the dark of Jacques' mind. If his captors, after holding one course all day long, could so speedily abandon it at sight of one puff of smoke; if, in so remote a region, they could take such precautions on the mere chance that some stray foe might be skulking near, wouldn't they lack enthusiasm in giving chase to a boy heading straight toward the enemy country? Wouldn't they, in pursuit, move more and more slowly the farther south they got? Mightn't they give up the chase altogether if the boy could keep far enough in the lead to gain the debatable boundary lands in safety?

Not that the thing would be *safe*, exactly. But after all Jacques might just as well run away as not. He had not the faintest idea where these men were taking him or what they meant to do with him. He had heard them hint in their council last night at his being a spy. And even white men show no mercy to spies.   No, if he should go, the dangers—and they were considerable, he knew—were probably not a bit worse than what lay before him if he didn't break away.   The thing was not to think about the danger—any more than you'd stop, shivering, on the bank of a river on a winter morning— but just plunge in.

Once the decision was made Jacques could have laughed aloud with relief.   He felt almost as happy as though he were already free, running southward to meet the Little Chief.   But of course his feet were still carrying him away and must go on for—he glanced at the sun, on his left side now, a ball of red just plunging below the trees—a full hour more of daylight.

He made his plans carefully.   He reviewed all he had learned of the southward country while chasing rabbits and turkeys with the Little Chief through the woods below the persimmon camp and on their several journeys with the young men down among the enemy towns.   Jacques believed he remembered just how the towns lay.   He ticked their names off on his fingers: Noisy Owl, Town-on-a-hill, Bawling Goose, The Corn Worm Town. . . .   He had long since learned to chart a course across country by the sun or the moon or the Seven Stars—the white men's Big Dipper—and by the way moss grows on the trunks of trees.   He had his bow and arrows.   He was a fair shot now and could kill whatever he needed to eat.

The sun was down at last.   And at last the daylight was gone.   They stopped and made a tiny fire of hickory bark which gives no tell-tale smoke.   They hung their

arms, each on a forked stick planted close by his un-
rolled sleeping-skins, ate their cold gruel, and lay down
to sleep.   The one with the crest of black hawk feathers
sat up to keep the first watch.

Jacques had cut some cedar boughs as though he
wouldn't be able to sleep unless he made a mattress under
his deerskin.   The sentinel watched his preparations,
contemptuously, Jacques thought.   When Jacques got
his bed made, he did not at once lie down, but lifted
his quiver and bow down from their forked stick and
sat a long while polishing his arrows.   Every now and
then the lone sentry glanced at him.   At last Jacques
put his arrows back into the quiver.   But he didn't
hang it up again.   He watched his chance; and, when
the sentry wasn't looking, he slid it, with his bow, between his deerskin mattress and buffalo coverlet.   His
little old French coat was already there.   The Indian
woman who had made his pack had, luckily, remembered
to put it in.

Jacques got into bed and there squirmed into the
tight-sleeved coat and got his quiver strap over his
shoulder.   His restless movements made the black
hawk feathers turn his way more than once, but the
buffalo skin and the darkness made a safe screen.   He
reached out in the dark behind him and drew into his
bed a plump little cedar-tree he had dragged up along
with the boughs of which he had made his bed.   The
tree was just as tall as he was.   He hoped it would look
no broader than he once the furry coverlet weighted its
roundness down.

Just as he got the tree straightened out alongside

him, the watchman by the fire got up and came toward him. Jacques' heart waited. But the man came no farther than a little heap of hickory bark he had earlier gathered to keep his fire up. He stooped for a handful of the bark and walked back toward the fire. While the sentry's back was turned, Jacques crawled on all-fours out of his bed. It was surprisingly easy. The buffalo skin settled back on the recumbent cedar with a mild sigh. In the shadow of a great oak Jacques straightened himself.

The sentry had faced about now. He was looking directly at Jacques' bed. The movement had not escaped his ears. The Indian shut off the firelight with his cupped palms and peered across the dark. Jacques realized anxiously that the little tree under the covers lay too still—but it really was about the right size. After a moment the sentry sat down again and lit his pipe. His tobacco was lightly perfumed with sweet-gum leaves. The smoke tickled Jacques' nostrils. He had to press his thumb and forefinger hard against his nose to keep from sneezing.

Jacques put a hand behind him to hold his bow and quiver tight and still against his back and stepped along the black tree shadow. He moved as cautiously as if he were walking a foot-log over a high ravine. At the farther end of his shadow bridge, he looked back. The sentry held his pipe-bowl cupped in his palms and was staring placidly down into the fire.

CHAPTER XXV

The Deep Forest

JACQUES had taken his bearings when they were entering this wood. He made his way out along the ridge which they had followed here. But once down in the open plain beyond, he altered his course and set off running. Glancing over his shoulder at the Seven Stars he veered sharply south-southeast. He came soon to a creek he had to swim. He tied his coat in a bundle on his head to keep it dry; and as soon as his shoulders had dried off, he hurried to put the coat on again, because the night was cold. During the first hours his way lay mostly through open plains. There he had the stars to guide him and after a while the moon.

By daylight it clouded up and began to rain. Jacques' coat got soaked. He rolled it up and strapped it beside his quiver where it beat like a lump of ice against his shoulders. His legs smarted under the stinging sleety pelting. The rain was very uncomfortable, but he was glad of it all the same, because it washed away his tracks as fast as he made them. He even dared to rest during the morning under a big magnolia. It was shadowy and quiet there as in the heart of a wide tent. The rain clicked and tapped on the hard evergreen leaves. The sound made Jacques realize how sleepy he was, but he couldn't risk going to sleep yet. He made a sparing meal of rainwater and clammy crushed corn while he rested and then pushed on.

The rain stopped quite suddenly when he was traveling through a wooded stretch of country—the very groves where the people had camped last fall when they were harvesting persimmons. The light of the sun came into the woods all around him. He couldn't see the sun itself but he knew that it was just going down by the color of the light and the length of the shadows on the wet brown leaves under his feet. All the trees, the evergreens and the ones that were bare, too, had a thin little trembling line of light around their trunks and branches like the crowns that sainted people wear in holy pictures. And through the shimmering quiet came sharp and clear the call of the first partridge Jacques had heard this season. It sent a thrill of spring through his heart to hear that quick cheery call ring out through the bright wood.

Before the sun faded he found nearly a capful of hickory nuts in a tree hollow where some prudent squirrel had stored them. And a dozen yards farther on, where the ground fell sharply away in a gully, he searched out a shallow cave-like depression under the red clay bank where he and the Little Chief had once spent a night. The floor of the cave was of clean white sand. And close against the bank, just as he had hoped, it was quite dry. There was even a smooth bit of rock embedded in the sand to crack the hickory nuts on. He hung up his wet things on some bushes and then he crept in on the dry sand and made himself comfortable.

While the light lasted he cracked the nuts and picked out the meats. Half the meats he stored with his corn meal, half he munched for supper. He brushed the hulls carefully into his cap to empty in the next creek he should come to, wiped off the rock, and dusted sand over it again as he had found it. Then he stretched out and slept heavily for several hours. He hadn't had all the sleep he wanted then, but he roused himself and once more went pounding on his way.

Somewhere about midnight, he had to cross a wide, low land thickset with big canes and shaded by dark overhanging trees. He lost all view of the stars and became confused. He got an idea he might be going exactly counter to the way he intended, not running toward the Little Chief at all, but back the way he had come. He even persuaded himself for a little that he could hear his pursuers whooping after him in the dark. And after he was sure it was just owls, his heart kept hammering in panic. He groped along the trunk of a tree and couldn't tell by feeling which was the mossy side. He stopped still in the blackness, sweat pouring down his legs. "I will be patient," he said. "I will stand as still as an animal until I know what to do."

As he stood there in the close forest, shivering, the blackness became less black and still less black. The pale light was sweet somehow like music when you hear it far off. He lifted his face. Through a hole in the ceiling of the forest, showed the silver edge of the rising moon. It pushed up and up. Before him opened a scene that was quite familiar. He remembered that old lightning-scarred hickory and the clump of ragged

blackberry bushes beyond it and the dimpled miry look
the ground had.   It was the salt lick where he and the
Little Chief with the young men last fall had watched
all night long for deer.   He wasn't lost.   He knew
exactly where he was.   He was even farther along than
he had hoped he could be by a second moon-rising.   By
another daylight, at this rate, he'd be nearing the debatable land between the two nations—for still, although
a journey of many days must yet lie between him and the
Little Chief, he refused to think of any danger but that
of being caught and taken back.

Just in front of him, a deer stepped soundlessly out
of the thick trees into the moonlight and bent its head
to lick the salty earth.   The deer had shed its antlers—
this was the season some tribes called the Moon of Dropping Horns.   The deer's head had a shorn, defenseless
look.   By noon to-morrow, I'll be where I can safely
cook the tongue and a slice of venison, Jacques told himself, and stepped forward in the moonlight feeling in
his quiver for an arrow.

A shadow on the ground under his feet moved slightly,
Jacques started back.   On a limb over his head crouched
a dark shape, settling its haunches and swaying to measure its spring.   Jacques' shoulders pressed back against
rough tree bark and his neck strained backward, as he
stared up, waiting.   The panther's passing made a little breeze go over Jacques' moist, upturned face.   The
panther lit directly on the deer's back.   The bleating of
the helpless deer cut the stillness.   The panther yelled
hideously, and far away through the swamp his mate
answered him.   Jacques slid his unused arrow into his

quiver and moved off backward, feeling his way from tree to tree with his hands outspread behind him.

The next afternoon he made a little hickory-bark fire and roasted a brace of partridges he had killed with his arrows. He felt that the danger of pursuit was almost past now, but he was careful to burn the bones and feathers anyway and even to brush up the ashes and scatter them in the next stream he came to. That night and the next he took more sleep.

He told himself that he was getting along splendidly. But he would have given anything for somebody to talk to. Once he thought he heard people near him. It was at his noon-day rest. He had finished eating and was lying back on the ground with his head on his clasped hands, looking up at oak branches just flushing over with warm buds as though a reddened cloud had got tangled on them. He was probably half asleep. Anyway he heard what he took to be voices close by. He sat bolt upright, not in alarm but in pleasure—by now he was sure he wasn't being followed and the Indian war by that time had got to seeming unreal to him. He just thought how nice it would be to meet people again and eagerly parted the undergrowth at his elbows. But he saw only a great bronze turkey cock gobbling to his hens, who were busily eating acorns and murmuring among themselves.

That same evening, coming out on the brow of a hill he looked over at a company of brown figures moving about on the bank of a little stream below—Indians he took them to be, not unnaturally, perhaps a wandering band of hunters. And the thought of fires about to be kindled, of roasting venison and friendly tale-telling was too much for him. He shouted at the top of his voice and went plunging down the hillside, but by the time he got down to the stream the brown company had melted into the dusk. Jacques crouching low was just able to make out that the tracks on the ground were made by deer's hoofs. He couldn't find the print of a single human foot, though he stayed there all night and searched again next morning.

The nights of course were the loneliest time. Once he was waked out of a bad dream by the sound of scream-ing. When he got wide awake he knew the screams were not human voices but only the crying of owls again, but it was unpleasant all the same. Often padding feet roved outside the frail barrier of his firelight. And there was scarcely a night he didn't hear wolves and foxes barking. One time, when he camped on the bank of a creek and had a fine supper of fish caught with a line made of twisted bark and a bird-bone hook, his fire died down in the middle of the night. An alligator writhed himself out of the creek and nuzzled the re-mains of the fish out of the leaves on the ground and crunched and gulped them an arm's length from where Jacques, roused suddenly, sat up staring in the pale starlight.

At last he came to an abandoned Indian village, a handful of crumbling huts with old cleared fields near them. Then he passed in a single day several hunting camps one after the other. Still he didn't see a soul. The third hunting camp, however, bore marks of hav-ing been used very recently. The shelters had fresh cut boughs on them, the charred lightwood knots among the ashes of the campfires had not been wet by rain, and posted on a tree was a scroll of bark with a notice painted on its inner surface. From the little pictures and symbols which the Indians used instead of written words, Jacques was able to make out that the camp had been used by a war party consisting of eight chiefs and principal men and forty warriors of the lower nation on its way north to collect scalps. Jacques must have passed quite near them. It was only luck he hadn't met them face to face, only luck he hadn't run shouting crazily full into the midst of them instead of into that herd of timid deer. He shivered as if a cold wind had blown suddenly upon him.

A day's journey beyond this place while he was drinking at a spring at sundown he heard girls' voices approaching through the woods. It was a pine wood and there was no undergrowth where he could hide himself. So he scrambled up a tree. The Indian girls—there were two of them—came to the spring and filled their water bags and then engaged in a childish romp. Gay and frolicsome as young fauns they spattered each other with spring water and laughed, and the tall one chased the other through the trees. It was a warm springlike afternoon. Violets were springing everywhere through the brown pine needles on the ground. Out at the edge of the pine wood yellow jasmin showered down from a thicket of small oaks. When the girls ran through it their dark shoulders brushed the flowering jasmin aside like a curtain and shook its fragrance into the air. They came back at last for their water-

bags, panting and choking with merriment and went off
as they had come.

Jacques knew now that he must be very close to the
uppermost village. He kept to his treetop till it began to get dark and then he came down and stole along
in the direction the girls had taken. The path led up
and around the shoulder of a hill. The village lay in a
hollow beyond. He could see every part of it spread
out below him in the twilight: the town-house, the house
like a temple with the scalp-poles before it, the square
with its fires and the big torches of bundled reeds just
beginning to blaze out at the corners, the scattered huts,
the people moving about among them. The drums
were going tum-tum-tum. Some of the scattered people shaped into a circle on the hard ground inside the
torches and began to move around and around, rising
and falling all together like waves tossing.

The beat of the chichicois they carried and the sound
of their plaintive chanting rose clearly to Jacques' ears.
But he had no impulse now to go shouting, and running
down the hillside, looking for somebody to talk to. He
crouched on the hill in the dark and looked down on the
dance a while and then he turned back into the woods.

The group of towns and villages of which this was
the most northern one lay thick-clustered across a wide
country. Each had broad fields skirting it and all were
connected one to the other with well-trodden trails with
people going and coming upon them. It was an open
and populous country, easy to get about in if you were
traveling openly, but correspondingly hard if you were
trying to keep under cover. Jacques made his way

alongside the trails, never upon them.   The trails ran
on ridges and high ground.   He kept to the lowlands
where there was more undergrowth to hide in and where
often there were creeks or streams which were so full
of water now that much of the time he could wade or
swim and so leave no footprints.   He traveled mostly
at night, getting through the towns.   He hunted no
more, made no more fires, but lived on the meal he had
saved and the nut-meats, of which he had now a considerable store stuffed in his meal pouch, in his coat
pockets, and even in the bottom of his quiver.

The town which the Little Chief's party would reach
first and which was therefore his own approximate goal
lay to the south and east of the others.   When Jacques
had got clear of all the rest and it alone lay before him,
he climbed a tall cypress and surveyed the country carefully.   The town ahead stood on high ground almost
hidden by trees.   You could just make out a thatched
roof here and there.   Stretching away along a southward ridge ran the trail over which the Little Chief must
pass.   A wooded creek bottom curved around the fields
lying on the slopes below the town.   Jacques' plan was
to maneuver for a sheltered position close to the trail
and station himself there to wait for the Little Chief.
He saw now that to do this he must skirt not only the
town on its hill but the wide bare fields as well.   It was
plain that the creek bottom, long as it was because of its
deep curve, was his safest course.

He slipped to the ground.   Suddenly he heard footsteps near.   He crouched quickly in the undergrowth
and, peering out, saw a man, who stopped and, to his

THE PEOPLE BEGAN TO MOVE AROUND AND AROUND.

horror, looked straight in his direction. The man, though painted and feathered like an Indian, somehow didn't seem like an Indian. He stared a moment at the bush behind which Jacques was huddled. Then he stretched his bow and aimed an arrow toward it. Jacques went crashing and stumbling away through briars and tangled vines. The man lowered his bow and gave chase, shouting.

Jacques managed to get away, but the incident unnerved him. He was full of terror all the morning, running crazily this way or that at the least crack of a dead stick under his own feet. He went miles out of his way to keep to the creek bottom and often he plunged in and swam under water till his head ached.

And then, suddenly, when he had crept out of the water to rest a little in a place where the bank was high and seemingly well sheltered, the terrible thing happened again. Only this time it was certainly an Indian who stood looking at Jacques' hiding-place as though the bushes that screened it weren't there at all. Any hunter would shoot into bushes if he saw them shake a little, Jacques told himself. I should myself. So this time, as soon as the man drew an arrow out of his quiver, Jacques, without waiting for him to stretch his bow or take aim, sprang up from his hiding-place and flung both arms high in air. He wanted to show plainly that he was a boy, not an animal to be shot at. The Indian's eyes met Jacques' squarely. He even smiled a little. Then he fitted the arrow against his taut bowstring and sighted straight along it.

Jacques dropped flat. As he pressed his pounding

breast hard against the ground the arrow whizzed above
him.   He crawled a few feet on his stomach, half rose,
ran crouching to the edge of the bank and slid off into the
water.

He stayed under longer than he ever had before.
And when he came up at last close beside a floating mass
of uprooted trees, drums beat in his temples and it was
minutes before his eyes cleared enough for him to search
the bank for the Indian who had shot at him.   Even
then, uncertain how far he had swum, he didn't know
exactly where to look.   By the time he'd got his bearings, there was no one in sight.   No use to tell himself
that he was nervous after his days and nights of loneliness.   That arrow had been real.   No use trying to
puzzle out why anyone should wish to do him harm.
A man had shot at him.   The man was still near lurk-
ing out of sight on the bank.   If Jacques should lift
his head above the mass of tangled roots and branches to
which he clung panting, he was sure another arrow
would whiz out at him.

CHAPTER XXVI

The Great Chief's Calumet

Major Boisbriant, coming up through country of the pine barrens, found every creek and river up. The Indians had to make rafts of bundled canes to get the French soldiers and their own new-bought treasures across. To Major Boisbriant, impatient to get a disagreeable job over and done with as quickly as possible, each ferriage seemed longer than the one before. Entering the enemy country at last, his charges openly lagged. As the scouts reported finding war signs stuck up on trees here and there, their uneasiness increased. Once at nightfall a certain uncommon little bird, which the Indians called the Kind-ill Messenger, perched in the trees over their camp and chirped fitfully. The

Indians promptly held a council; and a committee, including some of their boldest warriors, waited upon Major Boisbriant as he sat eating his supper by the campfire and announced to him that they would do no more scout duty.

Major Boisbriant, with such eloquence as his halting command of their language permitted, upbraided them for this, asking them how it was that men of a nation which laid claim to being the bravest of all Indian nations could be so weak as to be afraid the moment their feet trod enemy soil.   One of their chiefs answered promptly.   He said it was true that their nation was the bravest of all peoples, its warriors the fiercest and most invincible, and that they habitually trod without fear the soil of their enemies; but, he pointed out, that was when they went as warriors and men, springing through the forests alert as panthers stalking deer.

"Now our feet are slowed to the gait of our young and of our women whose corn carriers bear hard upon their shoulders with the weight of red and green beads and gaudy blankets.   It is for their sakes we go groping, afraid of thorns.   When we go as warriors we sip our cold gruel, take in our belts, and are content; but now the hunger of our white friends requires that we make every night great fires which the spies of our enemies can behold and report when they bound back into their towns, calling the news whoop before them as they go."

Major Boisbriant humored them in this as he had already humored them in so much during the long journey.   When it was morning he assigned his own men to scout duty, and the straggling column moved on.   The

day was fair and warm. The air was full of spring
odors. Many trees were putting out. The bottom
lands were perfumed with azaleas. Toward afternoon
they came to the enemy town which lay first in their way.

The people in the town did not interfere with them
or even speak to them as they passed in. The warriors,
reclining on skins before their doors, indifferently puffed
slow smoke into the spring sunshine. The women, busy
at cookery, skin-dressing and whatnot, merely stared a
moment and went on with their tasks. The young men
did not interrupt their game of the hurled stone discus.
In the square the great chief greeted Major Boisbriant
politely and at once led him into the council house.
There he listened with courtesy while the French officer
explained that he wished to pass up through the nation
with his friends.

"Your friends?" murmured the great chief. "You
would not call them so, perhaps, if you knew what has
happened to the young French boy trusted to their keeping."

Major Boisbriant's understanding of the language
was very imperfect. He was hardly sure that he had
heard the insinuation correctly. Even if he had, it was
the merest hint of course, and no doubt false. The
chief probably threw it off only to weaken Major Boisbriant's purpose to protect his charges—he'd be glad
to blacken his enemies in the eyes of the French. Major
Boisbriant decided to take no notice of the cryptic re-
mark. As if he hadn't heard it at all, he repeated his
request for permission to pass peaceably up through the
towns. The great chief then lit the calumet of peace

with its floating fan of white swan feathers, and puffing
it ceremoniously, handed it to his guest.

"To-morrow," he promised, "you shall go on your
way. To-night you shall rest here, and our women shall
cook for you. These people whom you are conducting
are not *our* friends—" here a slight smile touched his
lips—"but we shall give them food, too. It will even
be a satisfaction to me to have this opportunity of re-
hearsing to them the wrongs which I and my people
have suffered at their hands."

He rose to his feet and the interview was at an end.
In a few minutes after they came out of the council house,
the whole town was in a stir. The square was swept and
sanded as for the festival of ripe corn. Huge torches
of bundled canes were set up at all the corners. Fires
were kindled and the feast pots set to cook.

While this festal stir was whipping up, the visiting
Indians huddled together, silent and uneasy. The
French soldiers strolled up and down, guns in hand, but
whistling carelessly or chatting among themselves. A
young lieutenant accosted Major Boisbriant as he
walked restlessly about.

"Monsieur, Coudret is here in the town. Pierre
Coudret, you know, the redheaded Norman who deserted his wife. He wants to speak to you."

"That renegade," said Major Boisbriant, shrugging
his shoulders. "I don't care to have anything to do
with him." But before the lieutenant was fairly turned
away he called him back. "I'll see him," he amended.

"Yes, Monsieur."

The man Coudret was painted and tattooed and bedizened with feathers like an Indian. He wore no clothes but a deerskin breechclout dyed red. The only thing civilized about him was, oddly, a little copper crucifix, such as peddlers in France sold to devout peasants, hanging midway of a necklace made of bears' teeth strung together. Major Boisbriant eyed the fellow with distaste.

"Well?"

"That boy . . . I think his name's Duval, Monsieur . . . anyway, the chap who was sent up-country a couple of years ago . . . to learn to be an interpreter, I think, Monsieur—"

"Yes, yes," Major Boisbriant said sharply. "What do you know about him?"

"I saw him . . . I think, Monsieur."

"You saw him! Where was this? When? Quick. Speak up."

"Yesterday in the woods just above here. I saw something move through a sweet myrtle thicket, and I all but shot him for a bear. He ran, and I got a glimpse of his face, only a glimpse. I'm not sure it was Duval, but it was some white boy—and I don't know who else it could be. I hallooed and shouted but he wouldn't stop."

Major Boisbriant frowned. He was thinking hard.

"Did you tell the great chief about this?"

"No, Monsieur."

The man wasn't trustworthy, of course, but he seemed to be telling the truth.

"Then no one knows the boy's about but yourself?"

"Unless someone else has seen him, too, Monsieur."

Yes, of course. Coudret had seen him. Why not someone else? The chief knew of the boy's presence. Else why that sly hint about foul play?

"And this was yesterday?"

"Early yesterday morning, Monsieur."

"Thanks, Coudret. Your information is . . . ah . . . interesting."

Major Boisbriant turned away rubbing his palms one against the other nervously.

The great chief would not grieve if ill befell the French boy who had been trusted to his enemy's keeping. That was certain. If one of his own hunters taking aim at a bear should shoot the boy instead, the great chief could by insinuation make out a very good case against his enemies. Was the thing done already? It was too much to hope that any boy astray in these woods could long survive, once his head was in pawn to savage diplomacy. Major Boisbriant was a fighter. He didn't understand the tricks which, with these people, passed for statecraft. But he was beginning to. He called his lieutenant.

"There's a smell of treachery in this business. We'd better not put too much trust in the chief's promises. Pass the word among our men not to put their guns out of their hands even to eat. We must do our best to protect our charges. The men will have to take care of themselves, but keep the women and children together, and if there is trouble get them into the house assigned to me and station a guard over them."

"Yes, Monsieur."

The Indian boy who wore the gage of Bienville's no-

tice was the center of a group of soldiers.   One of them
pointed out to the others that the boy's gun, though
French, was not like those given in trade at the French
fort.   And another soldier who had picked up a few
Indian phrases asked the boy where he'd got it.   The
boy, having no words in his language perhaps to de-
scribe the fiddling carpenter or else thinking they
wouldn't understand him if he spoke, merely made the
gestures of a man playing a violin.   The soldiers
roared with laughter calling out to each other: "Picard
to the life.   Watch the chap nod his head and pat his
foot to keep time to the tune.   Isn't he the sharp one?
I'll bet his people make him the great chief a few years
from now."

The boy left his gun in their hands and nonchalantly
walked on his hands across the trodden square.   The
French snuff-box given him by Monsieur de Bienville
dangled down his ribs and swung back and forth like a
pendulum.   He gave Major Boisbriant a friendly in-
verted smile as the Major crossed the square.

As dark came on people collected from the other
towns to the most amazing number.   They gathered
slowly by one's and two's.   But there seemed to be no
end to their coming.   Converging on the flamelit square
out of the night, not talking, and moving on soundless
feet, they came on and on, until it seemed as though
the very leaves upon the trees were turning into men.
A soldier sent a startled glance across his shoulder.

"Mother of God!" he whispered.   "How many do
you think there are?   Three thousand?"

"Th-three?" echoed his fellow, a tall lout from

Gascony with a stammer. "My poor lad, it's nearer t-twelve."

At last the big torches were lit and the visiting warriors were invited to sit down in a circle in the middle of the square. The drummer seated himself, too, with his drum between his crossed legs and with his pounding called the dancers out. They came leaping and twirling their chichicois and singing. When the dance was over the great chief as host rose among the seated visitors holding in his hand the calumet he had smoked with Major Boisbriant in the afternoon. It was very beautiful. It had a carved bowl as big as a man's two fists. Its fan of white swan feathers hung down to the great chief's knees.

"You are a wicked and perfidious people," began the great chief, looking around at his seated enemies. "From the earliest memory of our forefathers you have inflicted injuries upon us."

He smiled almost benignly. His forehead, flattened from birth by sandbags, rose above his eyes to twice the height of a normal brow. Above that sheer and awful expanse towered, like pines above a cliff, the eagle feather coronal of his kingly rank. His smile, set off by fearful red and yellow scorings down his cheeks, was as inscrutable as a god's.

"The French, who are protecting you, call you their friends. Do you imagine they would do so if they knew that the young French boy they gave into your care is dead?"

There it was—in the open at last. A dozen startled questions fluttered up from Major Boisbriant's mind and beat helpless wings against the great chief's smooth and clifflike brow.

Behind the warriors, cross-legged on the ground, in the full light of the blazing giant torches a figure moved across the square. Major Boisbriant stared and crossed himself. Jacques Duval smiled faintly at the gesture and strolled up to him—at least *strolled* was the way Major Boisbriant thought of it, seeing the boy come along through the hostile throng careless as though he bore a charmed life. But to Jacques it hardly seemed like strolling. His feet dragged the ground as if his ragged moccasins had lead in them. It is no light matter to be hunted through the woods for two whole days like a deer or a rabbit.

In his panic he had lost the southward trail this morning. And, when he had come out on it at last, late this afternoon, the travelers had already gone by. He had missed them after all. He had seen the print of the French soldiers' shoes and a dozen other betraying signs such as white men always fling carelessly about to mark where they have passed. But that hadn't re-assured him: only the more people to be anxious for, don't you see? More of his friends in danger—and all because Jacques had lost his head and failed to be there to warn them.

After that, there had seemed nothing left to do but to come back and cast in his lot with his friends. So here he was, drifted into town unnoticed in the crowds and darkness. Blinded by the fires, he stood a moment, looking about for someone he knew. Then the chief's saying that he was dead seemed, vaguely, a thing he should do something about. So he stepped out into the light and came "strolling" across to Major Boisbriant.

"Maybe if you'd tell him that isn't true, Monsieur—"

Major Boisbriant, recovering from his surprise, shrugged slightly. He pointed to the great chief. Jacques turned. The great chief was looking straight at Jacques. He wasn't confounded at all by Jacques' presence. He smiled in that same curious way that made shivers of dread shoot down your spine.

And his eloquence rolled on.

"If I have been misinformed about the French boy's death, there are other things which I—and you, too, O venomous snake people—know to be true. You have raided our country. You have burned our houses. You have made slaves of our women and children." The red and yellow scorings beside the chief's mouth contorted with hate and his voice swept up like the blast of a trumpet. "You do not deserve to pass as peaceful strangers and honored guests. You deserve to die."

Suddenly the great calumet tilted in his hand. The swinging white fan turned upside down and its lining of flamingo feathers blazed red in the firelight. Major Boisbriant sprang to his feet. He shouted, "No, no, no." But if the onrushing hosts had been leaves whirled in a resistless wind they could have heeded him no less. He saw that nothing could stop them. He abandoned all attempt at protest. Turning his back on the seated warriors—doomed anyway, of course—he faced to-

ward the end of the square where the women and children were huddled together.

"Get them out of the way," he shouted at his soldiers.   "Get them out of the way."

The swift command was barely swift enough.   Panic
was already at work.   The women turned like crazed
cattle on the soldiers who were trying to save them.
Major Boisbriant ran in that direction shouting his com-
mands.   Jacques Duval stood alone in the middle of
the tumult, unable, it seemed, to move.   Only his eyes
moved, frantically searching this way and that for his
friend, the Little Chief.

As the French soldiers herded their flock, bleating
like helpless animals, out of the flamelit square toward
the shadows, a fox brush against a boy's naked thigh
flashed into view among the uniforms.   In the outer
nimbus of light, the wearer of the fox brush engaged in
a dim struggle with a French soldier, got free and darted
off.   Through the gap thus forced in the cordon a
woman, too, slipped out of the flock.   It was the woman
the soldier ran after.   He caught her and thrust her
back with the rest.   The boy wearing the fox brush
got away and went on running.   He ran full into
the light.   It was the Little Chief.   He was running
straight back into the square.

"You'll be killed, you young idiot," yelled Major
Boisbriant.   "You'll be killed."

"Go back, Little Chief," screamed Jacques Duval,
able to move at last.   "Go back!"

He ran in front of his friend to head him off.   Major

Boisbriant gave chase, too. The Indian boy swung out in a wide arc to elude them. He cleared with a bound a heap of spread-out mats and half-emptied platters where a moment before some people had been eating supper. He darted away in the dark. He dodged in and out behind trees, brandishing his gun and calling: "I am not a child! I am a man, I am a man!"

Once Major Boisbriant almost caught him. He actually had his hands on him, but then the gun in the Indian boy's hands went off. The charge blazed into Major Boisbriant's side, and he staggered, clutching the broken lid of a French snuff-box. In that instant the French boy seemed to him as mad as the young Indian, for he would have followed the other straight into the death-swept square. But, as Major Boisbriant's knees buckled, he managed to fling his arms around the white boy's legs and, with the weight of his falling body, to pin him struggling to the ground. The naked young Indian, slim and feather-crested, darted toward the firelight, poised at the edge of the red, seething caldron like a diver on the brink of a cool river, and then plunged from sight.

CHAPTER XXVII

Broadcloth and Buttons

A RAGGED sentry walked up and down before the gate at Fort Louis and saw day break. A mist lay over everything. A herd of lean-flanked cattle huddled at the far side of Place Royale, dim as phantoms. The rigging of a sloop which lay in the river showed gossamer, like spiders' weaving. The cypresses in the swamp across the river, steeped in fog and mist, were mere floating genii. From their unseen summits a wild turkey cock shouted and was answered by roosters in the settlement. Out of the woods into the clearing drifted a straggling troop of ghosts. The sentry interrupted his even pace and stared. One of the ghosts, with its arm in a sling and weary bent shoulders, passed close by the sentry, and the sentry peered into its face.

"Mother of God! It's the stammering Gascon. You must have had trouble up-country then?"

"A b-b-bloodier bit of it than any Christian wants to be mixed up in."

"Anybody killed?"

"Anybody k-k-k—! Say—did you ever see a massacre?"

"Who's that on the litter?"

"Major B-b-boisbriant."

"Badly hurt?"

"N-n-nearly well. It's been a fortnight now."

The last of the dreary parade was passing. The Gascon ambled after it. A boy straggling at the very end stopped beside the sentry.

"Can you tell me if Picard the carpenter is back yet? The soldiers said he went upriver the night before they started."

"He did—and he isn't back."

"But it's a *month* since then! He ought to be—"

"He ought," agreed the sentry. "But for the matter of that a man ought not to strike off alone into an Indian war if he doesn't expect to be—delayed," he finished with a sinister intonation.

A rooster straddling past stretched his wings and crowed. The sentry spat at the rooster. The spittle ran down the rooster's eyes, and he made a fussy henlike noise in his throat as he ran off. The sentry laughed.

The mist was lifting now. Blossoming dogwood in the woods about the clearing prickled alight. Above the thatched roofs it looked like fresh lace at the edge of a ragged sleeve. There were no tents now, only houses. Breakfast smoke was beginning to come out of the chimneys. A young woman whom Jacques had never seen before came out on Place Royale with a stick in her hand and drove one of the cows before her. She disappeared driving the cow along the little street which had been marked Rue de Boisbriant on Monsieur d'Iberville's map, and turned into the one that had been Rue de Tonti.

"Will you tell me which is Marie's house?" Jacques asked the sentry.

"Do you mean Mademoiselle Marie Le Sueur the cousin of Monsieur de Bienville, or Marie the cobbler's wife, or—"

"I mean the wife of Pierre Coudret who ran away to the Indians last year."

"Oh—Mad Marie. Well, don't look at me like that. You know yourself it's mad to begin watching the river again for a man that's been gone a year and a half and wringing one's hands and muttering to oneself. Eh, is it mad or isn't it?" Jacques making no answer to this, the sentry asked: "Have you some message for Marie from her fine husband up in the Indian country?"

Jacques held up a necklace of bears' teeth with a copper crucifix hanging to it.

"He was killed," he said. "I wanted to give her this."

The sentry took the trinket on his palm. He seemed to find the crucifix and bears' teeth amusing to look at. He laughed out loud.

"So Coudret's dead. Well, well. Wouldn't you like me to give this to Marie? I'm going off duty in a few minutes now. I'll be passing right by her house. I can hand it in to her easily. I'd like to see her face when she hears her fine husband's dead. What do you say? Shall I save you that trouble?"

"If you like," said Jacques, and turned away indifferently.

He walked off along the bluff. He walked a long way and when he came back near the fort again he saw

a pirogue come upstream and tie up at the little wharf.
All the heads in the pirogue were feathered—a party of
Indians from some tribe westward along the Gulf Coast,
Jacques supposed.   He idly watched them get out of
the pirogue and climb the bluff.   They were almost upon
him before he recognized them.

"How did you get here?" he cried out.   "How could
you come *up*river?"

The man with the crest of black hawk feathers answered.   They had gone west to the Mississippi and
then by pirogue down the great river, around the Gulf
Coast, and up.

"It was the way we had planned to bring you in safety
to your friends."   The Indian's voice was sad with reproach.   "But you did not trust us.   After living with
our people for two years and experiencing only kindness
from them, you did not trust us.   You trusted instead
the panthers and wolves of the forest and our cruel
and bloodthirsty enemies."

It was hopeless to try to explain.   So much had happened.   It was unlikely they knew yet about the massacre.   The weight of that gloomy secret made Jacques
hang his head.   The Indians kindled a fire there on the
bluff, and Jacques turned away without a word.

He passed inside the open gate of the fort.   The
sun was bright now.   The flag whipped at the blue sky.
Back and forth across the parade ground people hurried on the business of a new day.   The commissary's
son sat on a bench before the king's warehouse whittling
at a bit of cane.

"I say—hello!"

"Hello."

"Maybe you don't remember me?"

"Oh, yes, I remember you."

"Why, what have you done with your buttons?"

"My buttons?" Jacques looked down. He had on no shirt. Besides deerskin moccasins and breechclout, indeed, he had on nothing at all but an old blue woolen coat much too small for him. The pocket of the coat was ragged where it had been burned long ago. The sleeves reached only a little below Jacques' elbows. The lapels were pinched together across his naked chest and tied with a scrap of deer sinew threaded through the buttonholes. The coat had no buttons. But of course it had had buttons once. Jacques frowned. "Oh—we shot buffalo with them," he said at last.

"Oh, come now, you don't expect me to be so green as all that. You couldn't put a button in a gun and shoot it!"

"No. We melted them into bullet molds first."

"O-o-oh." There was something like respect in the tone. "Whom do you mean by *we?* And how many buffalo did you kill?"

"I'd rather not talk about it."

"Did you see the massacre?"

"Yes."

Silence.

"I'm a cadet now."

Then Jacques noticed that the commissary's son had on a new military uniform trimmed with braid and buttons.

"That's fine," he said and tried to smile.

"Father!" The cadet leaned around on the bench and shouted into the warehouse. "Here's young Duval, Father. He saw the massacre."

The commissary came out and shook Jacques' hand quite heartily. The smoke of the Indians' fire was rising now above the log wall of the fort. The commissary asked what that might be. Jacques told him.

"Well, they're lucky to get here alive," the commissary commented. "It's a pity Monsieur de Bienville did not send their kin home around by the Mississippi, too."

Jacques started. *It needn't have happened.* The Little Chief needn't have been killed if Monsieur de Bienville had been careful—like the chiefs and warriors who had set out to bring Jacques safely back. Jacques felt his lips whiten. It was as if the real pain were just beginning.

"Come inside and have a sip of wine," said the commissary with surprising kindness.

There was a priest writing at a table. He moved along his bench to make way for Jacques, and the commissary set out a glass and poured wine into it. The commissary's son pushed it toward Jacques and smiled.

"You're a funny boy, Duval—not wanting to tell about the buffalo you killed or the massacre or anything. You've always been funny like that. It was funny your traveling all the way across the ocean with me and letting me think you were just a ship's boy and never once telling me you were coming over here to live with the Indians and learn to be an interpreter."

"I didn't know it myself."

"You didn't know it! You mean your people didn't
tell you when they signed up for you?"

"They—my father it was—didn't know it either."

"Did you hear that, Father?" the cadet asked the
commissary. "Fancy Monsieur d'Iberville taking
Duval and not telling his family what he was being let
in for."

"I'm not surprised," said the commissary dryly, and
as he poured Jacques' glass full again he glanced at the
priest. "You might put that in your letter to the king
—bringing people over under false pretenses."

The priest nodded and went on writing. The commissary sent his son to get a bowl of sagamité for Jacques.
But Jacques wasn't hungry. He couldn't swallow anything but wine. A woman came in to ask the commissary if it was true that letters for France could go on
the sloop sailing to the West Indies. He told her it
was. Then a soldier brought the commissary a note.

The commissary read the note and said:

"I will tell him." As soon as the soldier was gone
Monsieur Nicolas turned to Jacques. "Monsieur de
Bienville orders you to report to him in the government
house at once. He wants you . . ." The commissary
paused, smiled with a certain bitterness . . . "to go out
with him on the bluff and break the news to your Indian friends about that little affair up-country."

"Ah—" The cry broke in Jacques' throat.

The priest spoke for the first time.

"Why should the lad be the one to have to tell them?
Why doesn't Monsieur de Bienville tell them himself?"

Jacques knew when the commissary went out, but he

didn't pay much attention. The wine had begun to make him feel warmer and the priest talked to him politely. The commissary's son was polite, too. He seemed to admire Jacques although, while he himself wore a fine military uniform, Jacques was dressed more poorly than a beggar would be in France.

After a while Monsieur Nicolas came back. He had a sheet of paper in his hand. He laid it down before Jacques with a flourish. But the wine had made Jacques feel sleepy, and the words all ran together under his eyes. The priest had to read the paper to him. It said that Jacques Duval, listed on the king's payroll as a ship's boy, was hereby honorably discharged from the king's service and was free to go aboard the sloop which was sailing to-morrow morning to the West Indies and thence, by whatever ship availed, to France.

"To France," cried the cadet. "Do you hear that, Duval?"

Jacques looked from one to the other of them.

"Why am I discharged?"

"Because," said Monsieur Nicolas with a wink, "you expected to be simply a ship's boy. You didn't expect to become an interpreter. Monsieur de Bienville doesn't wish to be unfair to you."

Monsieur Nicolas sent a bitter smile in the direction of the priest.

"Duval can't go home without clothes," the cadet reminded.

"Certainly not," agreed Monsieur Nicolas. "A suit came for him on the *Pelican,* I think. I can sell him shirts and stockings, of course. He can have whatever he likes. The king is in his debt for two years' pay. Have you got anything to pack some clothes in, Duval?"

"I have a sea chest, Monsieur, at Picard's house—wherever it was he lodged when he was here."

The commissary's son ran to get Jacques' chest.

Everything seemed, curiously, to have happened before, but, like printed pages turned backward, made no sense. Jacques watched the commissary packing clothes for him to go to France. And he told the priest that he was going to study Latin when he got home. But the whole thing was unreal. At last he put on a new outfit of linen and broadcloth with glittering buttons and went out by himself.

CHAPTER XXVIII

If the King Would Give Me Paris

JACQUES walked slowly across the parade ground. On spread-out skins in a circle sat the newly arrived warriors and chiefs and the French officers, Monsieur de Bienville looking startlingly older than when Jacques had gone away and Major Boisbriant white and haggard from his recent wounds. Evidently the bad news had just been told: the Indians' faces were heavy with sorrow and Monsieur de Bienville was frowning anxiously. But Monsieur de Bienville's perplexities were no business of Jacques' now. Jacques was discharged. Jacques was going home to France.

He went out of the gate, crossed the scrabbly grass of the absurdly named Place Royale, to the edge of the bluff. A sloop lay anchored in the river. Her sails were patched and dirty. Her hull needed paint. It looked as if worms had been at it, too. A ragged barefoot sailor was coming ashore in a rowboat.

"Hey, ship's boy!"

He was one of the old crew of the *Palm Tree*. Jacques returned his greeting and smiled faintly. The sailor tied up at the wooden wharf, climbed the bluff, and trotted off in the direction of the fort. In a few minutes he was back with a bale of skins. Were the skins of Jacques' and the Little Chief's kill in that bale perhaps? The sailor made three trips between the wharf and the fort. The last time he brought Jacques' chest on his shoulder. The red and black anchor painted on the tarred canvas showed from far off in the morning sunshine. The friendly sailor hailed Jacques again as he came by with the old chest.

"So we're to be shipmates again?"

"Yes," said Jacques. "I'm going home."

"I guess there's many another in this colony wishes they could say the same."

"I guess so."

The sailor put the chest atop his load, untied the rope, and pushed off. Jacques watched the sailor row out to the sloop and watched his own chest being hoisted up over the side.

So this was how it ended.

The Little Chief was dead—without his war name. And Jacques, having done nothing at all, was going home. Picard and his gaily singing violin were lost in a red whirlpool of war. Marie was mad. Monsieur Bosset hadn't lived long enough even to build his inn. The

Iron Hand, after all his brave deeds, had died of a fever in his bed. Monsieur d'Iberville was ill in France. Monsieur de Bienville wasn't getting his desires very fast by the look of him. He looked old and worried. Did he know about the priest's letter to the king? He must know that the priest was on the commissary's side —and that the royal commissary hated him. And those warriors and chiefs in there on the parade ground now weren't going to forgive Monsieur de Bienville in a hurry. Why should they?

A sorry business. Jacques was lucky to be out of it, lucky, as the sailor had said, to be going home.

He conjured a picture of himself sitting on a bench in a walled garden. The garden was filled to the brim with warm, fragrant sunlight, like a glass with wine. Jacques saw himself sitting in the shade of the tree called the Mainmast. A cat lay curled on his knees and he was stroking it. Aunt Gabrielle on a stool by the kitchen door was peeling peaches for conserve. The smell of the peaches mixed with the smell of the roses in the sun. The skipper came limping down the graveled path and nodded at Jacques as he let himself out of the gate. His halting step went along the street outside the wall in the direction of Little Sailor Inn. Aunt Gabrielle got up clasping the wooden platter of peeled peaches against her waist and went indoors. The sun tilted over the wall. Across the garden floated the sound of sweet bells ringing.

Jacques' eyeballs smarted. Why, what was the matter with him? Wasn't he glad he was going home?

Aunt Gabrielle would be very happy. She must have missed having Jacques to fuss over, to wash for and mend and cook for. And the skipper, too, would be glad to see him. The skipper liked tales of the New World better than any others. Jacques wasn't a child now. He could sit with the skipper and his friends sipping wine and talking. . . .

A remembered sweetness breathed upon the air, like a fragrance but not a fragrance. A thin whisper of music that quivered, fainted, and died. Marie heard it—Mad Marie. She came running across Place Royale, her old blue cape blowing out behind her. She passed right by Jacques without seeing him. Again that whispered sweetness, nearer now, almost tangible:

> If the king would give to me
> Paris, his big city . . .

Jacques leaned out over the edge of the bluff looking upriver. A little pirogue paddled by two Indians floated into sight. A cap like a big red rose nodded over the pirogue and under the nodding cap a violin was singing gaily:

> I'd surely say to the king—
> Keep you your big city,
> I'd rather have my love, thanks,
> I'd rather have my love!

Jacques could not spring off into the river and go swimming to meet Picard as once before. A rickety wharf stretched below the bluff, and Jacques had on too many clothes now. Anyway, Marie was going to be the one to welcome Picard this time.　She scrambled down the twisting red clay path, catching at a leaning yaupon bush to steady herself.　Jacques caught a glimpse of her face as she turned.　Marie mad?　Why it was Picard she'd been watching for!

She was leaning over the edge of the wharf when the pirogue tied up.　As soon as Picard got his two feet on the planking, Marie opened her palm and showed him something.　Was it a bears' tooth necklace with a crucifix dangling?　It seemed to be.　Picard solemnly crossed himself, shut her fingers up over the thing on her palms, and then bent and kissed her gently.　They came up the path not speaking a word but clinging together.　When they saw Jacques standing there on the bluff, they both cried out.

"You here, old fellow?" Picard exclaimed.　"Your friends up-country told me an escort had started home with you the long way around.　I hardly supposed you'd be ahead of me.　How's the Mississippi—full, I guess?"

"I didn't come that way," Jacques began and then he stopped.

There was such a lot Picard didn't know yet. Jacques didn't know what to tell him first.　Besides, Marie had run to put her arms around Jacques and something that had been frozen inside of him threatened to melt.　He freed himself hastily from her soft arms.

"I'm going home," he blurted.

That was beginning just backward.　He ought to have told about the Little Chief first.　Then they'd

have understood better why Jacques was going. Their
cries of astonishment, their gestures had—or he imagined that they had—a flavor of reproach.

"I should think you'd be glad of my luck," he began
again defensively. "It's pretty nice, I think." He
held out the paper which said he was discharged.
"Monsieur Nicolas got it for me."

Picard suddenly withdrew the hand he was putting
out toward the paper. He never had liked Monsieur
Nicolas of course. He said:

"Marie's going to give me some sagamité. I've had
nothing but raw onions for days. Come along,
Jacques?"

He didn't call Jacques "old fellow" again or crinkle
up the leathery skin around the corners of his eyes in a
smile. Jacques shook his head.

"I'm not hungry, thanks."

They walked off without looking back. Jacques
hadn't said one word about the Little Chief. He stood
a moment wistfully fingering the paper in his hand. It
was hard to feel that Picard and Marie were disappointed in him. But no matter who disapproved he
was going home. He couldn't bear to stay now.

Jacques wandered back into the fort. On the parade
ground Monsieur de Bienville, speaking in a persuasive
tone about the benefits of peace, was describing some
country—Jacques thought at first it was France—where
men felt so secure that they sang as they worked in their
broad fields. Even in the forests like deep green parks
they hunted only deer and other game, never each
other. In the rivers and bays, ships and boats were as

thick as people feasting in a public square. In the towns and villages, sown like corn across the land, each house stood in a garden and there were churches with carved steeples and sweet bells ringing.

Jacques had been listening some minutes before he realized that Monsieur de Bienville wasn't talking about France. He wasn't talking about a real place at all, just an imaginary one, the one he wanted to make here in the Indians' country. It sounded a little crazy—especially to anybody who knew what this country really was like: twisty rivers, treacherous swamps, tangled woods bristling with every sort of danger. . . . But of course Monsieur de Bienville and his fantastic dreams were nothing to Jacques one way or the other now. Jacques was going home.

The Indian with the black hawk crest got up next. He passed over Monsieur de Bienville's fairy tale and made a bitter speech aginst the white men:

Why did the French come into our country? We did not go to seek them. Were we not better off before their coming? What occasion had we for Frenchmen? Was it for their guns? Our bows and arrows made us live well. Was it for their red and blue blankets? Our buffalo skins were warmer. Our women wrought for us, besides, shining feather mantles, for winter and white cloth of mulberry bark for summer. Did we need vermilion or little tinkling garter bells to pamper the vanity of our young men? Before the French came our young men thought more of getting their war names than of painting their bodies and hanging their thighs with trinkets. Our warriors went into the enemy's country to bring back scalps, not to be murdered sitting about the feast pots.

The Indian orator shaped his climax to an open hint that Major Boisbriant had purposely led their kindred into an ambush. He paused a moment then, evidently expecting Major Boisbriant to leap up and repudiate the insult. But Major Boisbriant was fidgeting with his sword hilt as though it hurt his wounded side. He didn't even look up. He didn't understand the Indian language very well. Maybe he had failed to catch the insinuation of treachery. It had been very subtly put. But it was bad, bad for the charge to go unanswered. The Indians took the major's silence for an admission of guilt. Jacques knew they did. He knew exactly what the Indians were thinking as they all lowered their eyes and sat looking at the ground. He dug his nails against his palms in sudden intense anxiety. It surprised him that he could care like that—when to-morrow he'd be away from it all.

The man with the black hawk feathers smiled curiously and resumed his speech. He repeated the soiling imputation in another form. He made it a lot bolder. Still Major Boisbriant fingered his sword. But Monsieur de Bienville looked up. As the Indian stopped abruptly and sat down, Monsieur de Bienville said in a surprised voice:

"He accused you of treachery, Boisbriant!"

Major Boisbriant shrugged.

"Why, that would be absurd. I didn't need to go all that distance to destroy his kin. We had them here in our power, didn't we? Besides, you've already explained that my soldiers saved their women and children at risk of life and that I was wounded myself trying to save one of their youths. You must have misunderstood him, Bienville."

Monsieur de Bienville happened to glance in Jacques' direction. Jacques ran up to him.

"Oh, Monsieur," he cried without stopping to think, "you didn't misunderstand. It *was* an accusation of treachery. He said it twice over. And when Major Boisbriant doesn't deny it they believe it's because he can't. They all think he wouldn't keep silent if it weren't true."

Monsieur de Bienville smiled slightly but he turned to Major Boisbriant all the same and said:

"The boy's right. It's slander. You'll have to resent it, Boisbriant."

Major Boisbriant rose painfully, his lips twisting in irony.

"If they think I'm guilty now," he murmured, "they'll know it when I begin to stutter and stammer."

It was true. He didn't use the Indian language at all well. Whenever he tried, his utterance was slow and uncertain. Monsieur de Bienville frowned.

"Speak French," he said suddenly. "We'll have young Duval here interpret. He understands them well now, it seems—what they say and even what they're thinking."

He smiled again.

"Oh, Monsieur . . ." Jacques stammered and flushed.

Monsieur de Bienville took no notice of his confusion. He got up and stood by Jacques side.

"Ready, Boisbriant?"

"Quite ready, thanks."

"Ready, Duval?"

"Yes, Monsieur."

Major Boisbriant's speech was short, too short, Jacques feared. But it was sharp and straight like the major's sword. Jacques repeated it to the Indians exactly. At the end they lifted their eyes from the ground and looked at the man who wore the black hawk feathers. He was lighting his pipe. He took one puff at it and then offered it to Major Boisbriant. Monsieur de Bienville turned to Jacques and smiled.

"Too bad you're going home, Duval. You might have been very useful to us."

Jacques caught his breath. It was noon now. The tattered flag hung like any old meaningless bunch of rags downward on the pole. The peeled pole had got quite gray and old-looking in these two years. Nobody, not even Monsieur de Bienville, could make Jacques stay here and be an interpreter if he didn't want to. His fingers at this moment gripped fast the paper that said he was discharged. His chest was already aboard the sloop. The sloop would sail to-morrow morning. Home. The walled garden. His father and Aunt Gabrielle would have been so glad. . . .

Monsieur de Bienville glanced at the paper Jacques handed him.

"You haven't changed your mind!"

"Yes, Monsieur—if you please—"

Monsieur de Bienville tore Jacques' discharge in two and shook hands with him quite warmly before he sat down to receive the pipe, which Major Boisbriant was

ready to pass on.   The Indians' tobacco was lightly
perfumed with sweet-gum leaves.   It tickled the nostrils pleasantly.   Through the open gate of the fort
across the Place showed the houses with the dogwood
sprinkled white as snowflakes along their ragged
thatches.   Far away out of sight Picard's violin was
humming an old French love tune.   A redbird poised
at the tip of the gray weathered flagpole and began to
sing.

Indians

Indians suppos[ed]
to be canniba[ls]

Louisiana
1702

Henry C Pitz
1930